The Wicked Marquis

Blackhaven Brides
Book 5

MARY LANCASTER

Books from Dragonblade Publishing

Knights of Honor Series by Alexa Aston
Word of Honor
Marked By Honor
Code of Honor
Journey to Honor
Heart of Honor
Bold in Honor

Legends of Love Series by Avril Borthiry
The Wishing Well
Isolated Hearts
Sentinel

The Lost Lords Series by Chasity Bowlin
The Lost Lord of Castle Black
The Vanishing of Lord Vale

By Elizabeth Ellen Carter
Captive of the Corsairs, *Heart of the Corsairs Series*
Revenge of the Corsairs, *Heart of the Corsairs Series*
Dark Heart

Knight Everlasting Series by Cassidy Cayman
Endearing
Enchanted

Midnight Meetings Series by Gina Conkle
Meet a Rogue at Midnight, book 4

Second Chance Series by Jessica Jefferson
Second Chance Marquess

Imperial Season Series by Mary Lancaster
Vienna Waltz
Vienna Woods
Vienna Dawn

Blackhaven Brides Series by Mary Lancaster
The Wicked Baron
The Wicked Lady
The Wicked Rebel
The Wicked Husband
The Wicked Marquis

Highland Loves Series by Melissa Limoges
My Reckless Love

Clash of the Tartans Series by Anna Markland
Kilty Secrets
Kilted at the Altar

Queen of Thieves Series by Andy Peloquin
Child of the Night Guild
Thief of the Night Guild
Queen of the Night Guild

Dark Gardens Series by Meara Platt
Garden of Shadows
Garden of Light
Garden of Dragons
Garden of Destiny

Rulers of the Sky Series by Paula Quinn
Scorched
Ember
White Hot

Highlands Forever Series by Violetta Rand
Unbreakable

Viking's Fury Series by Violetta Rand
Love's Fury
Desire's Fury
Passion's Fury

Also from Violetta Rand
Viking Hearts

The Sons of Scotland Series by Victoria Vane
Virtue
Valor

Dry Bayou Brides Series by Lynn Winchester
The Shepherd's Daughter
The Seamstress
The Widow

Table of Contents

Chapter One

L ADY SERENA WALTZED into the schoolroom. Finding herself in a beam of bright sunshine, she halted and winked at her younger sisters. For their entertainment, she created bird-shapes with her hands that reflected on the opposite wall. Maria grinned, Alice chortled, and Helen actually sprang to her feet in instant desire to make shapes of her own.

Miss Grey swung around on Serena, clearly irritated.

"I know, I know," Serena exclaimed, throwing up her hands in submission. "I'm sorry, I'll go,"

She *was* sorry, too, for she rather liked Miss Grey, who was quite young with twinkling eyes, and not at all like the governesses she and her older sister Frances had endured. Hastily, she left the room, ignoring Helen's pout of disappointment. Clearly, she'd made Miss Grey's job just a little harder today.

Sighing, she walked restlessly from the schoolroom along the passage to the long gallery and from there, into the large drawing room, where she opened the lid of the pianoforte and spread her fingers on the keys.

Without making a sound, she let her hands slide off into her lap. She didn't really want to play. She wanted to run.

In truth, she still felt aggrieved. She was being punished for the faithlessness of Sir Arthur Maynard, to whom she'd been engaged until very recently, when after several weeks of sulking and petulance, he finally insisted she break off the engagement. The ending of the betrothal everyone had been so proud of had actually come as a surprising relief to Serena.

Until her mother and brother united in anger and sent her home to Braithwaite Castle in disgrace—with the children and their governess, to add insult to injury. Not that it wasn't fun spending more time than usual with her younger sisters, but they had plans and lessons and routines. Serena didn't. And she was bored.

Her eyes strayed to the window. She didn't normally see the castle grounds in the autumn, and the rich reds and golds were rather beautiful, especially in the afternoon sunshine.

Wishing she could take a walk outside, she rose, just as a figure in the garden below caught her attention. She thought, at first, he must be a new gardener, for he wore a long, disreputable old coat and carried a satchel over his shoulder as well as something large under his arm. But on closer inspection, his burdens didn't look much like tools of any kind. Still, he must have had some purpose here, for he didn't appear remotely furtive as he strolled along the path toward the main part of the castle. In fact, he was whistling. She could hear the faint strains of his merry tune drifting upward and see the purse of his lips as he raised his head and looked about.

Serena's heartbeat quickened with interest, not so much at his undeniable good looks, but because he had one of the most fascinating faces she had ever seen. Framed by too-long, wild black hair, his features were dramatic—a long, slightly hooked nose, thick eyebrows, full lips—and his expression somehow at once unworldly and sardonic.

He spun around and stopped whistling. When she next glimpsed his face, it seemed vaguely dissatisfied, though with what she couldn't tell. In any case, he strode on again, veering off the path to the side door and heading toward the orchard instead.

Intrigued, Serena seized her shawl from the back of an armchair and made her way outside. She had always known she would never keep to her mother's strictures not to step out of doors, even in the castle grounds, without company. Especially when the company was restricted to her sisters, Miss Grey, or Mrs. Gaskell the housekeeper. No old friends from Blackhaven were permitted. It was a ridiculous requirement, and bad for her health, as even the countess her mother would agree once she had stopped being so angry.

In fact, it would be bad for everyone else, too, for being so trapped was already making Serena crazy and disruptive. So, she would go and disrupt this new employee instead, whoever he was and whatever he did. That would pass ten minutes or so. More, if he proved to be as interesting as he looked.

She passed a maid in the passageway that led to the orchard-facing side door. The girl only curtseyed. So at least the servants weren't aware of her humiliating restrictions.

Fresh air hit her with a bolt of joy. After a week of being cooped up in a travelling coach, and more than half of another spent inside the castle, it was wonderful to be outside, reveling in the sharpness of the air and the warmth of the sunshine on her face.

She all but skipped along the path to the orchard, forgetting what and who had tempted her outside in the first place. Once through the orchard door, she closed it and ran full tilt up the hill. She whirled around the biggest apple tree and spread her arms out to rush back down the hill, just as she'd used to with Frances and Gervaise when they were children.

Then, breathless and much happier, she rearranged her shawl and walked more sedately along the sun-dappled path through the trees toward the top gate from where she could reach the woods.

"Stop!" a voice commanded, freezing her instantly. "Don't move."

"Why ever not?" she demanded, her mind flitting around possible dangers like snakes, tree branches about to fall, and fox traps left where they shouldn't be.

"Just hold very still," the same, deep male voice said gently, as though he were speaking to a startled horse. But she could hear the quick tread and rustle of his approaching footsteps. Then he halted.

Serena waited. "What are you doing?" she asked.

"Committing this to memory," he said, and began to move again.

The hairs on the back of her neck prickled as he came closer. He brushed past, his face turned toward her and came to a halt once more in front of her.

His black hair gleamed in the sunlight. His gaze was rivetted to her face, his expression rapt, a faint, fascinating smile curving his lips. The interesting employee who'd first drawn her outside.

"Who *are* you?" she demanded. "Do you work here?"

"I try to," he replied. "Do you?"

"Not exactly." He didn't know who she was. Well, she'd dressed in her oldest, most comfortable dress, discovered with delight at the back of her wardrobe, and she didn't really look like the daughter and sister of earls. For some reason, such anonymity felt truly liberating.

In fact, he didn't seem remotely interested in names. Instead, he continued walking around her.

"This is marvelous," he enthused. "And the light will never be quite like this again. No!" He seized her shoulder when she started to turn, shocking her into awareness. "Don't move a muscle."

Half-amused, half-annoyed, she subsided, and he released her to dash back the way he'd come. She heard the swishing of tree branches, the squeak of hinges, and his returning footfall, quick but slightly heavier, as though he was carrying something.

She waited for a few impatient moments. Then, unable to resist, she glanced back over her shoulder.

He stood a couple of yards behind her, an easel in front of him, painting with a small, narrow brush at what seemed a furious rate. His eyes darted constantly from his canvas to her, then he began to frown. "Look straight ahead. Don't take a step. Please," he added with a quick, distracted grin.

"Hurry, then, for I can't stand here all day," she retorted, slightly piqued that anyone should prefer the back of her head to the front. But she did face ahead again.

He didn't speak, and she found herself wondering what it was about the light that so entranced him. Shining through the trees, it did have that pretty, dappled quality on the ground at least, and she could imagine the muted, autumn colors of the leaves and hills beyond as part of a fairy tale world.

"I always found it frustrating," she remembered, "that I could never paint what I saw. Frances and Gillie were always better than me."

"Did *they* paint what you saw?"

"No. I always itched to change them—or make *them* change them, for I'd just have spoiled their paintings—but they never knew what I was talking about."

"So you're never satisfied with anyone's painting," he observed.

"Well, I haven't seen yours yet," she pointed out, eager to see what he did with the red of the falling leaves.

"It will probably be a long wait."

She sensed movement behind her and again her skin prickled in a way that was not remotely unpleasant. In fact, it was oddly exciting. He appeared in front of her, a sketch book and pencil in his hands, staring at her face until she felt a blush rise under his scrutiny. She could only suppose the view was better from the back. And then his pencil flew across the page. A faint smile played about his lips as he worked.

"There," he said, lowering pencil and paper, and striding back to his easel.

She swung around to watch him pack his things into the satchel and the bundle she'd seen him carrying from the drawing room window. "May I not see?"

"If it turns into anything half-way good. Walk with me?"

Serena blinked. "Walk with you where?"

"Anywhere. I'd like to know something of the young lady behind the beautiful face."

"It's too late for flattery," she said severely. "I already know you prefer the back of my head."

He smiled. "It's all you."

Somehow, they'd fallen into step together, walking along the orchard path in the direction she'd meant to take before he stopped her.

"You don't work here at all, do you?"

"Well, I do occasionally," he insisted, patting his satchel. "But no, I am not employed in the Earl's household. What's your name?"

"Serena." Now, surely, he would recognize the name and know she was the Earl's sister. Inevitably, his over-casual manners would change, whatever class he came from, and that would be a shame. She rather liked him as he was.

Certainly, he regarded her more closely, almost as if he were surprised. "It's a pretty name," he allowed. "But you don't seem terribly serene to me."

"I'm not," she said ruefully. "I'm in disgrace."

"Why?"

"My engagement has been broken."

"By you?"

"Officially," she confessed. "But in fact, he did it."

The artist gazed at her, frowning faintly. "What a fatwit."

"Yes, but he's been more than generous in allowing me to do the crying off and so save what's left of my reputation."

"Good Lord. What on earth did you do?"

She sighed. "Nothing. I danced three times instead of two with Lord Daxton, but only because we both forgot. And," she admitted in the interests of honesty, "I may have flirted with him a little."

"Well, he's a fun person to be with. I'd probably flirt with him myself if the circumstances were right."

She laughed. "You say the oddest things."

"I'm a pretty odd person."

"Do you paint as a living?" she asked curiously.

"Not sure it would count as a living. It lets us eat but doesn't keep the bailiffs off my back."

"Us?"

"Siblings," he said disparagingly.

For some reason she was pleased he hadn't meant wife and children. "Do you have many siblings?"

"Two brothers, two sisters, but one of the sisters is married, thank God. You?"

"One older brother, one older, married sister, and three younger sisters." She frowned. "Why do you paint at the castle? There are better views in the environs of Blackhaven, surely, than this orchard."

He cast her a sardonic glance. "Did I mention the bailiffs? I'm hiding."

"Really?" she said, intrigued all over again.

"Sadly, yes."

"I'll tell them you've gone to Scotland, if that would help?"

"It might," he said, gratefully. "Thank you."

"We might need the rest of the town to tell the same story, of course, but... Are you laughing at me?"

"I'm delighting in you, which is quite different."

She cast him an uncertain glance. His teasing was verging on flirting, which she really couldn't allow, especially given her disgrace. Besides which, he was a stranger of whom she knew nothing, and an artist to boot. She doubted anyone would consider him respectable let alone safe.

"It's a good thing and quite harmless," he assured her, reaching up to pluck a solitary leaf off an apple tree branch. It was pale, golden brown and, halting his step, he held it up to her hair. "Almost."

"Almost what?" she asked, bewildered.

"The same color."

"Is *that* good?" she asked with a hint of defiance.

"Exact would be better," he said. "For the leaf."

She couldn't help smiling. "You talk a lot of nonsense, you know."

"So I've been told." His gaze dipped from her eyes to the region of her lips, and her breath caught.

"I should go." Although she meant it to be decisive and forbidding, the words sounded as reluctant as she felt about leaving the eccentric stranger just yet.

"Must you?" He sounded flatteringly disappointed. Slowly, his gaze lifted back to hers.

He had rather beautiful eyes for a man, large and dark and yet always with that shade of laughter, as if he was never serious about the world. They caused a thrilling little twist in her stomach, as though a flock of butterflies had just taken wing.

She swallowed. "Yes, I must," she said firmly.

"Then meet me again tomorrow."

I can't.

"Here?" he suggested.

She raised her eyebrows. "If you're still hiding from your bailiffs."

"Until tomorrow, then." He raised his hand to her cheek, his fingertips just brushing her skin. A smile flickered across his lips and was gone as he lowered his head.

Her heart turned over, for his intention was obvious. She couldn't allow this… But if she'd ever truly meant to avoid it, he was too quick. His mouth fastened to hers, gentle and sweet and melting. Her eyelids fluttered shut, and then it was over.

He raised his head, waiting, it seemed, for her reaction.

"Why did you do that?" she blurted.

"Well, I don't often get the chance to kiss the women I really want to paint."

She frowned. "I don't know if I should be insulted or flattered."

"Neither. I never flatter, you know, and I'd certainly never insult you. Until tomorrow."

Forcing herself, she hurried away from him. At the end of the path, she couldn't help turning back, but he'd already gone.

RUPERT GAUNT, THE impoverished Marquis of Tamar, walked back to Blackhaven from the castle with his vision full of the girl, Serena. She'd intrigued him first by the way she ran up the orchard hill and spun around with the sheer joy of living. There had been such energy in her, such a sense of escape and freedom that he'd found himself smiling. And then she'd run down the hill again before assuming a much more sedate posture that had almost made him laugh out loud.

And then the sunlight caught her hair and he'd had to stop her, to catch the image before it faded. She wasn't just beautiful, she was enchanting...

He shouldn't have kissed her, of course. That was hardly gentle-manly, however chaste the embrace. She'd just looked so lonely and sad and confoundedly sweet that he'd acted on instinct—which generally turned out badly for him. But she hadn't thrown a fit of the vapors, and her lips had been deliciously soft...

Vaguely aware of people greeting him in the street as he strode through town, he merely lifted one hand in response, for he could not stop.

He lived in a small cottage by the shore, and as he turned onto the front road leading to it, he caught sight of Rivers, the bum-bailiff hastening up the street toward him. With aplomb, Tamar darted into the nearest cottage doorway.

Fortunately, the door was open.

"Sorry," he muttered, diving inside.

The gentleman known as Smuggler Jack, nodded amiably at him from the table in the middle of the room, where he seemed to be mending a fishing net. "Law after you?"

"Bailiff. Wants money or intends to haul me off to debtors' prison. Not sure which would make him happier."

Jack rose to his feet and ambled to the door, where he inhaled deeply and stretched. "He's been hanging around all day, sitting on your front step." He glanced up and down the road. "He's heading up toward the tavern now."

"Thanks, Jack. I owe you."

"Any time."

Tamar clapped him on the back and stepped past him into the road. Then he strode on toward his own cottage, which he called his studio.

Entering, he carefully locked the door behind him, but he was reluctant to close the shutters and block out the light. Hopefully, Rivers had gone for the day.

Tamar threw his coat on the floor and set up his easel among the mess. He propped the canvas up on it and gazed at Serena's beautiful hair in the dappled sunlight, shining and pretty. He *had* caught the color of the light, which had been his most urgent concern. Now he could finish it at his leisure.

Bending, he took the sketch book from his satchel and examined the hasty pencil sketch of her face. He could do a pair, Serena the un-serene beauty, front and back.

Smiling, he fetched more paint and began to mix.

Chapter Two

"*I DON'T OFTEN get the chance to kiss the women I really want to paint.*" How many women, exactly, *did* he kiss—or want to kiss!

Even lying in bed, several hours later, she could still feel the soft pressure of his lips on hers. The kiss made her glad and tingly all over, and she really, really didn't want to imagine she was one of many. She *refused* to be one of many. Which was why she had to pull herself together. If she ever encountered him again, she had to be distant enough to repel such familiarity. He would be a fun friend—if she could keep him secret from the household. A friend who neither took nor received the liberty he had today.

She should be angry with him. She would be, she thought, if he'd actually known who she was. He probably imagined her to be some maid, or perhaps the governess, which didn't entitle him to liberties either, of course. But even the most rakish of gentlemen would think twice about offending the Earl of Braithwaite. And truly, she hadn't given him much reason to doubt that his kiss would be acceptable.

Oh dear, he would think her a lightskirt! Although not perfectly sure what such a female did, she was sure it entailed granting kisses to strangers, and it was assuredly *not* a good thing to be.

Boredom, it seemed, was doing terrible things to her. Why did her mother and brother not realize this would happen? After all, it was boredom that had led to her flirting with Dax in the first place. How much more bored was she likely to get being stuck up here with nothing to do but distract the children from their lessons and placate Miss Grey with Cook's treats from the kitchen?

In any case, when she met the artist again—*if* she met him again—in the orchard or anywhere else, dignified friendliness was the attitude she should aim for. And she had to tell him exactly who she was.

Her mind made up, she closed her eyes once more and found herself remembering his kiss. Which was a rather lovely way to fall asleep.

She woke with a thud, unsure if what she'd heard had been in her dream or in reality, or even if it was just the beat of her own heart.

But then she heard movement outside, a rolling, scraping sound in the old courtyard below her window. Hastily, she rose and felt her way to the window and pulled back the heavy curtain.

It was another clear night, the moon and stars illuminating the scene below like a vignette in a book. Two men and a barrel.

Smugglers. Hardly a rare sight around Blackhaven. Serena was aware they used Braithwaite Cove below the castle to land their contraband, though these days they generally only did it when the family was not in residence. She was fairly sure her brother received a generous amount of French brandy for his discretion, and he certainly wasn't the only one in Blackhaven. Even the knowledge that many smugglers were now in the pay of the French didn't stop the trade altogether.

What did surprise her was that they should have brought their goods this far up to the castle. In the old days, a keg or two of brandy was left on the beach below, or at the castle gates. It wasn't right that they should treat her family's home as their contraband store, however seldom any of the family were in residence these days. She should have a word with them...Gillie's friend, Smuggler Jack, perhaps. Or her brother Bernard would surely know what was going on.

Sighing, she let the curtain fall back and padded back to bed.

SERENA SLEPT ONLY fitfully for the rest of the night. She kept waking up, disturbed either by actual comings and goings or by her imagination. In the end, she gave in and rose early. Having washed and dressed—in a rather newer day gown of fine wool to counteract the castle draughts—she went in search of her sisters. They were discovered in their beds, all still sound asleep. Even Miss Grey was only just waking up, yawning owlishly at her when she stuck her head round her bedchamber door.

"Slugabeds, all of you!" Serena accused and went off to the kitchen instead to beg some warm, freshly baked bread from Cook. Cook cut her a thick slice and slathered it in butter, handing it to her with a tolerant wink and an apple.

Serena hugged her and danced off with her treasure, pausing only to seize her warm cloak on the way out the door.

It was going to be another beautiful morning. As it was, the sun hadn't quite risen, and there was a hint of frost in the crunching of the grass beneath her feet. Serena considered breaking her confinement altogether and walking into Blackhaven. Only Gillie, her childhood friend was not there but with her husband at Wickenden where she awaited the birth of their first child.

Who would have thought it? The last time Serena had been home, it had been Gillie who was in disgrace, and Serena who'd won the brilliant match, or at least a respectable one. And yet here she was back on the marriage mart, while Gillie had everything.

Not that Serena begrudged her it, for she loved Gillie very much, and her friend's wicked baron was a lot more exciting than Serena's wealthy baronet. In fact, Gillie was a living lesson, that marriage needn't be dull and constricting.

While thinking about Gillie, Serena's footsteps seemed to have led to the orchard. She laughed at herself, for it was far too early to expect any visitors, let alone the eccentric artist. Besides, it would not do to be seen *waiting* for him.

As her hand stilled on the latch of the orchard door, a sound in the distance drew her attention and she glanced along the wide formal garden that ran along the orchard wall to the old courtyard entrance. Someone stood there, half turned away from her, apparently calling to someone else inside the courtyard.

Frowning, Serena released the latch and hurried toward the court-yard instead. There was no real reason for any of the servants to be there, except to go to the wine cellar, which was extremely unlikely at this time of day. It crossed Serena's mind that the man was not a Braithwaite servant, but a smuggler, and if so, he needed to under-stand where the boundary line was drawn. She would not report their activities or even put an end to them—after all, most of the town was complicit to one degree or another. But smugglers could not be running tame about the castle.

As if he heard her footsteps, the man glanced around, saw her, and immediately bolted inside the courtyard. She'd been right. He was no servant. Picking up her skirts, she ran after him, but when she reached the courtyard, there was no sign of anyone at all. And the cellar, when she tried the outside door, was locked.

Were they on the inside? Her blood ran cold. Were they running loose about the castle? Were they *living* here? Surely, the servants would be aware of such a thing. Walking into the middle of the courtyard, she gazed up at the windows, including that of her own bedchamber, and turned to those disused parts on the left-hand side. On the third side was merely an ancient wall, partially ruined and rebuilt, in which a newer, cast iron gate had been added. And it seemed to be ajar.

She darted toward it, but before she even swung it open, she saw through the bars, the unmistakable figure of a man bolting into the woods.

Well at least he's not inside the castle, she thought with relief, hurry-ing after him. She opened her mouth to yell to him to stop, before it struck her that neither of them really wanted to draw attention. She ran faster, and was rewarded when, from the line of trees, he glanced over his shoulder and saw her.

She waved. But rather than waiting for her, her quarry simply delved into the trees and vanished.

"Oh, for the love of—" But no, he was being sensible. They would talk where no passing gardener would notice them.

When she reached the spot from where he'd seen her, there was no sign of him. Peering through the trees all around her, she crept forward, twigs crunching and snapping beneath her feet.

"Hello?" she hazarded and then, getting no response. "I need to talk to you, but I'm not here to threaten."

Twigs crackled to her right, drawing her further in. And then, when she was just about to give up, a man stepped out of the trees—surely the man she'd followed from the courtyard—and he lunged at her. He'd have caught her, too, if her reflexes hadn't been so quick. She leapt back beyond his reach and bolted in sudden terror, for she'd glimpsed the glittering steel in his hand. He didn't want to talk. He meant her harm.

As she ran through the trees, she heard him pounding after her, crashing through the undergrowth. But it was hard to locate him now, for she kept changing direction in an effort to fool him and her heart thundered too loudly in her ears, eclipsing everything but her own desperately panting breath.

Branches moved to her right and she swerved left, thudding into a hard, male body. Hands seized her. She made a pathetic sound in her throat that she'd meant to be a scream and lashed out at the region of his chest with her balled fists. His grip only tightened.

"Hush, I'm not going to hurt you," a soothing and familiar voice said.

The artist.

She gasped, her hands opening and clutching his coat in her relief. "On thank God it's you! I thought..."

"What did you think?" he asked. He held her comfortingly in one arm, but he seemed to be looking over her head, scouring the surrounding trees.

"There's a man," she said urgently, "a smuggler with a knife, a dagger of some kind. I don't suppose you're armed, sir, so we should flee!"

"Discretion is certainly the better part of valor," he agreed, still scanning the woods. "Although you should know I am the very devil with a stick." As she finally lifted her puzzled head from his too comfortable chest, he seized what looked like a trimmed branch which was propped up against the nearest tree, and made swift fencing motions with it. "See?"

"I see that you are just as mad as I remember," she said shakily.

"No, no, it's a perfectly sensible defense," he assured her, still with his arm around her shoulder as he began to walk with her toward the edge of the wood. "Only why is a smuggler attacking you?"

"I followed him from the castle," she confessed.

"How do you know he's a smuggler?"

She frowned. "Who else could he be? I saw them last night, hiding barrels in the castle cellar and that is not something Braithwaite would approve of, so when I saw him again this morning. I tried to tell him so, only he wouldn't stop to talk and then he just lunged at me, with a knife."

"Good God," the artist said, casting her a startled glance. "He actually *attacked* you?"

She nodded. For some reason, with his large person at her side, his arm around her, it no longer seemed too scary.

"Did he hurt you?"

"No, my reflexes are quick. Too many games of tag when we were children. I was the champion."

"Excellent practice for life, tag," he murmured. "Um, are you acquainted with this man?"

She shook her head. "I've never seen him before in my life."

"Well they do say, the "gentlemen" are no longer gentlemen. Bonaparte has made it a much dirtier business than merely avoiding duty. We should go and visit my neighbor, who knows about such things."

"Who is your neighbor?"

"His name is Jack and he and his family have a cottage on the shore, just a few yards along the street from mine."

"Smuggler Jack?" she said in surprise.

"With such a well-known name, I'm surprised the authorities

haven't clapped him up."

"Well, the authorities are local, too," she pointed out as they emerged from the trees. "Besides, I think Jack might have retired from the trade. The excise men shot him a few months back and his wife works for the Muirs now."

He cast her a glance sparkling with sudden amusement. "You are surprisingly knowledgeable in such matters."

His laughing eyes would be her undoing. She became aware of his nearness, of his unconventional escort with his arm still warm around her shoulders. Whatever had happened to the dignified friendliness she's been so determined to show him? Wretched smuggler.

Trying to squash the silly butterflies in her stomach, she drew away from the artist until his arm fell casually back to his side. He didn't seem to notice.

"Well, the Muirs are friends of mine," she said hastily. "Gillie Muir is now Lady Wickenden." That should give him some warning of her status at least.

"I know," he said.

She blinked. Well, everyone in town must know of Gillie's brilliant marriage. All the same, his words brought to mind something he'd said yesterday, after she'd mentioned her troubles stemming from flirting with Lord Daxton. *Well, he's a fun person to be with. I'd probably flirt with him myself.*

Daxton had a lot of odd and quite unrespectable friends. She shouldn't be surprised that one of them should be *him*. But it was now more urgent than ever that he understand her position.

With a very deliberate carelessness, she said, "You do know, then, that I am Serena Conway, Lord Braithwaite's sister?"

She wasn't quite sure what she expected. Possibly a blanching of his face, or a look of horror, almost certainly an apology for his familiarity to call it no worse. And a change in his manner that she would, in spite of everything, be sorry for.

But the artist only smiled faintly, without much obvious interest in her words. "Yes, I know."

She blinked. "You do?"

"Well, yes. It didn't register just at first, but you seemed so at home here and there had been talk in town of your arrival at the castle."

"Then...then it does not...*bother* you that I am Lady Serena?" she demanded.

At last, his eyebrows rose in surprise. "Of course not. It's who you are."

"Like the back of my head?" she said with a hint of tartness.

He grinned. "The back of your head is very charming, your nape delightful. I'm sure you already know how beautiful you are from the front."

"You are outrageous!" she exclaimed.

"If you mean I should apologize for kissing you, I'm afraid I can't regret that, for I liked it excessively. On the other hand, if I offended you, I *am* sorry—I meant it to have the opposite effect."

Speechless, Serena merely stared at him, though laughter seemed to be rising up from her stomach. Perhaps she was hysterical.

"About your smuggler, though, you need to involve the magistrate, or the soldiers, or both. You can't have armed strangers running tame about your home."

"I know, and I ought to inform against them, only first I need to get rid of whatever they're hiding in the cellar, or Braithwaite will get the blame."

He veered across toward the orchard, which was a short cut to the castle from this part of the wood. "Well, let's go and see, now. I can help your servants shift the contraband elsewhere—or tip it into the sea, which might be better."

She stopped in her tracks at the orchard door, catching his arm. "No, no, you can't come to the castle!"

"I can't?"

"I'm not allowed to receive male visitors, for my only chaperones are my sisters, Mrs. Gaskell the housekeeper, and Miss Grey the governess. In fact," she confided, "I'm not meant to receive any visitors at all. I'm not even meant to be outdoors."

Opening the door, he paused, frowning down at her. "Because you danced with Dax?"

She sailed past him. "Because my engagement to Sir Arthur is ended. No one can hold Dax responsible for that. It is my fault."

"Sounds like Sir Arthur's fault to me," the artist said disgustedly, his long, easy strides catching up with her. "I think you had a narrow escape and are much better off being *not* engaged to him."

"Well, to be frank, I have felt rather relieved," she confided, strolling along the path. Then her breath caught. There was something too comforting about the orchard walls, or perhaps it was the artist's large presence. "Oh drat, I'm doing it again."

"What?"

"Blabbering," she said ruefully.

"I shall be discreet enough for both of us," he assured her. "Our main problem is your smugglers."

"Well surely they won't come back now they know I've seen them?"

He made a noncommittal noise. "Is there direct access to the rest of the castle from the cellar?"

"No, it's quite inconvenient, actually. Braithwaite keeps talking about moving the wine cellar elsewhere, but so far, he hasn't. The only entrance is through the door in the old courtyard."

"So as long as your staff lock the rest of the doors, you should be safe?"

"Yes," she agreed, "although it must be said they lock the cellar door, too."

His frown deepened. "Then, our smugglers have at least one key. Serena, you have to go and stay somewhere else. Get your own people to move the contraband if you won't allow me, and then report this to—"

"I'm not leaving," she interrupted. "This is my home. Besides, if they haven't murdered my servants, why should they go out of their way to murder me?"

"Because the servants don't chase them through the woods?" he suggested.

"Well," she said, allowing him the point. "I expect they won't come back, for they'll surely expect to be confronted by excisemen, soldiers, and magistrates."

"I suppose it depends if they were merely leaving brandy for his lordship or up to something else entirely."

"What else could they possibly be up to?"

"I have no idea, but this behavior does not seem natural for Blackhaven smugglers."

She mulled that over and had to concede he was right. "Then, if you would be so good as to consult with Smuggler Jack on what is going on, I shall investigate the cellar."

"Do you have a *very* large footman employed at the castle?" he asked.

"Why?"

"Take him with you," the artist advised.

"Perhaps you'd lend him your stick?" she said innocently.

He narrowed his eyes. "Don't mock me, madam, or I might be forced to kiss you again."

"You can't kiss me again!" she all but gasped. "I'm the Earl's sister."

"You were always the Earl's sister."

She dropped her gaze before the dangerous glint in his. "You are most improper, sir."

"I suspect that's why you like me."

"I'm not perfectly sure I do like you," she retorted.

"Well, take my advice and don't go around kissing men you don't like."

She glared at him in outrage until she saw the laughter in his eyes. "You are impossible," she said crossly. "Do you take nothing seriously?"

"Actually, yes, but you don't pay attention when I'm serious."

His care for her safety was genuine, at least. Touched, she assured him she had a household full of devoted retainers. "And I'm sure Miss Grey could reduce twenty armed men to obedience," she added. "They'd probably be improving their letters before they escaped."

He laughed, and she thought there might be a hint of admiration in his smiling eyes. "You're not afraid of anything, are you, Serena?"

"How can you say that when you've just seen me terrified?"

"It was very temporary, and understandable to the point of being necessary to survival." He took an old-fashioned pocket watch from his coat and glanced it before giving it a shake. "Wretched thing's stopped again," he said, shoving it back in his pocket. "You don't know what the time is, do you? I have a hopeful worthy wanting to sit for his portrait at nine o'clock."

"It can only be around eight," Serena guessed, "but the gardeners will be abroad soon. You should go."

"The gardeners are mostly used to me."

She regarded him. "You are quite...insidious, aren't you?"

"You make me sound like a plague."

"I'm not perfectly sure you aren't. This castle was in perfect order when I left in the spring, and within a few months, it's become rife with smugglers and artists and I don't know who else. Bailiffs, probably, looking for you!"

"Don't say that," he begged.

"Are they still after you?" she asked with more sympathy.

"He sat on my doorstep all day yesterday, but I crept in when he left, and out before he came back."

"Is that why you're here so early?"

He smiled into her eyes, depriving her of breath. "No, that's because I wanted to see you."

"Stop that," she said severely. "And go and paint your worthy portrait. Goodbye!"

Before he could have any chance of repeating his outrageous behavior of yesterday, she hurried down the path toward the bottom door. He didn't follow.

However, her triumph was short-lived, quickly drowned in relentless disappointment. Truly, she would have liked him to kiss her again, whatever resolutions she'd given herself away from his company. And she should, in all decency, have thanked him for his support against the armed smuggler, for she was sure it was his presence that had scared the villain away. As well as being curiously *necessary* to her at the time.

She paused and turned back. He still stood where she'd left him, the familiar satchel over one shoulder, the stick still by his side. She lifted her hand in a wave and smiled with relief when he waved back.

With gladness now, she began to run down the rest of the hill, just as the bottom door opened and a large man walked in.

She skidded to a halt.

"Morning, m'lady."

It spoke volumes for her earlier fright that it took her so long to recognize an old childhood friend.

"Why, Jem! How are you?"

"Very well, m'lady. Good to see you home."

"It's good to *be* home," she assured him, and it was true, despite her annoying confinement. "How is your mother?"

"Keeping busy. She asked to be remembered to you, should I happen upon you."

"I'll call on her," Serena promised.

He smiled and raised his rake in salute. "She'd like that."

Jem, whom she'd once beaten at tag, had grown into a big, strapping young man. "Jem?" she called after him. "When you've finished here, could you help me with something else?"

Chapter Three

L ORD TAMAR TRIED to find the best in his sitter. A wealthy mill owner, he had a strong, determined face, and if there was also ruthlessness in the set of his lips that could turn quite easily to cruelty, there was challenge in that. Tamar was normally quite happy to paint the middle-aged, the old, or the ugly, who were often more interesting than the young and handsome. But today, he had no interest in any painting except the one in his studio that he'd begun yesterday. Lady Serena Conway.

But this was his bread and butter and he had to force himself to go through the motions. It was not his most productive hour, but he did make some progress and made a hasty arrangement to come back two days later, before he departed and strode homeward.

Rivers, the bum bailiff, was marching up and down the shore road, presumably to keep warm. When the man's back was to him, Tamar hastened after him and dived into Smuggler Jack's cottage.

Several children were wrestling on the floor, making such a racket that he didn't see how their father could possibly sleep through it. But, stretched out on the floor before the stove, Jack seemed to be managing.

"Morning Mr. Tamar!" called one of the children, half-emerging from the pile on the floor, a greeting echoed in a more muffled fashion by his siblings. "Can you wrestle Wee Jack, can you?"

"Right now, I couldn't wrestle the tiniest Jack who ever lived. Is your father sick?"

"No, he's resting his eyes. Will I wake him for you?"

"If you wouldn't mind," Tamar said.

The child pulled himself out of the sibling pile, rather like a man dragging himself from a swamp, and shook his father roughly.

Instead of the angry, or even violet reaction Tamar expected—for he could smell the alcohol from where he stood—Jack merely opened one eye.

"What?" he demanded.

"Mr. Tamar wants you," the child said cheerfully and threw himself back on top of his siblings.

"Who?" Jack said, hauling himself into a sitting position and shaking himself like a dog before peering owlishly around the cottage and discovering Tamar. "Ah, it's you. Just leave your things at the back, out of harm's way."

"Thanks, Jack. I wanted a word with you, too, if you're not too bosky."

Jack seemed to think about it, then shook his head. "Slept it off," he pronounced. He raised his voice. "Oi! Go and play outside!"

Somehow, the pile of children fell apart and bolted out of the doorway with cries of careless farewell flung at their father and Tamar.

"They're lively," Tamar observed.

"Weren't you at the same age?"

"Lively, yes, though I seem to remember it a lot more ill-natured. Jack, do smugglers use the castle to store contraband?"

Jack blinked at his bluntness. "How would I know that?" he demanded, getting to his feet and throwing himself on to a chair at the table instead.

"Jack. I need to know."

Jack scratched his head. "Cargo gets landed at Braithwaite Cove, especially when the family's not there, but you'd be stupid to leave it at the castle—any more than a couple of kegs for his lordship, that is. Stupid to leave it anywhere. It'd be gone too quick."

"You mean it's distributed immediately?"

"Long-standing customers," Jack explained.

"And are the—er—free traders hereabout long-standing, too? Same gentlemen as always?"

"Well, we had a bit of trouble some months back, nearly brought the soldiers down on all of us. And Captain Alban's ships passed by a few weeks ago, but they're long gone."

"And now?" Tamar pursued.

Again, Jack hesitated, Clearly, it went against the grain to talk about anything in the present.

"I wouldn't ask," Tamar said. "But something's going on at the castle and someone connected with it threatened Lady Serena."

"Threatened her?" Jack repeated quickly. "You mean to scare her off? Discourage her from meddling?"

"Well, frankly, that would be bad enough. You can't go around scaring innocent people. But in this case, no, he attacked her with a knife and chased her when she ran. If I hadn't chanced upon her—or if there had been more than one of them around at the time—I'm pretty sure she'd be dead."

He spoke with deliberate brutality, because he wanted Jack to face the truth of who he was covering for. But whatever his words did to Jack, Tamar's own blood ran cold.

"You can't go round killing earls' daughters," Jack said severely.

"No, you can't," Tamar agreed. "So you see why I'm worried and need to know."

Jack tugged at his hair. "There was a strange boat landed at Braithwaite Cove night before last. Landed several barrels. But no one bought from them. No one who buys from the usual gentlemen knew anything about them."

"So, they *are* storing them at the castle. Why would they do that?"

"Waiting until supply's low, then undercut us? I don't know. Unless they're Braithwaite's own men? But then they wouldn't try and kill his sister, would they?"

"I would hope not," Tamar said faintly. "So you've seen and heard nothing of these characters?"

Jack thought. "Not me, I haven't. Maybe at the tavern, though. There's always strangers, there. I'll spread the word, so they know they're not welcome."

"Thanks, Jack. Let me know if you hear anything else?"

"Aye, I will."

Tamar wasn't convinced he would, but it was the best he could hope for at the moment. Nodding amiably at Jack, he walked to the door and peered out.

Beyond the children now playing tag with a gaggle of other urchins who'd appeared from nowhere, Rivers was strolling in the direction of the market.

Keeping a weather eye on him, Tamar called to Jack's children. "Think you can distract that gentleman so that he doesn't see me going home?"

"Aye, easy!" came the reply, and while Tamar stepped nimbly along the street, the crowd of children roared in the opposite direction. When, fitting his key, he glanced after them, they'd surrounded the bewildered bailiff and seemed to be spinning him in circles.

Grinning, Tamar let himself inside and bolted the door behind him. As he threw his coat on the floor as usual, he caught sight of the two portraits he'd begun yesterday, and smiled. What he really wanted to do was throw himself in front of them and paint until the light vanished. But he needed to get Rivers off his back, and to do that, he needed to sell more pictures.

He'd had a run of sales at the Blackhaven gallery where he exhibited some of his paintings, but foolishly, he'd sent the money back to Tamar Abbey to feed his siblings—who were probably all sponging off his sister Christianne anyway. He knew he should go home and see what was happening there. In fact, he'd fully intended to do so this week, only now there was Serena to paint. After that, he would go. If he could stay out of debtor's prison.

Impatiently, he walked the length of his studio, looking for pictures to take to the gallery to sell. The trouble was, he never really considered any of them finished. Although there was the one of the harbor…

He pulled one landscape back from the wall, to pick out the harbor scene beneath. It was no longer there. Mildly irritated, he looked through all his other paintings in search of it. He scowled, trying to remember if he'd already sold it or given it away while he was foxed. Perhaps he'd already taken it to the gallery. He needed a damned assistant to take care of such things. Which would just be another expense he couldn't afford.

Shrugging, he picked up four landscapes at random and wrapped them in the old blanket he used for such purposes. Outside, the children were now marching up the street with the bailiff, engaging him in conversation. He seemed to have softened slightly.

Tamar shrugged his coat back on and waited until the bailiff was escorted in the other direction. Then he nipped outside, locked the door, and sprinted the opposite way along the row, taking the back lanes up to High Street.

Oddly enough, shameful as the whole thing might be, he imagined the hide and seek game with the bailiff would be a lot more fun if Serena was with him.

AFTER LUNCHEON WITH her sisters and Miss Grey, Serena extracted the wine cellar key from the housekeeper.

"Lord Braithwaite wanted me to count the bottles of a particular wine for him," she lied blithely, "and I shall be writing to him today." After all, there was no point in frightening her or the rest of the household—at least not until she knew what the devil was going on.

The housekeeper removed a key from her belt. "Be sure to give me it back at once, if you please. For Paton has mislaid his key and this is now the only one we have."

"How did he mislay it?" Serena asked at once.

"Who knows?" Mrs. Gaskell said tartly. "If we did, we could find it again."

"True," Serena said as if she didn't care, and tripped off to the courtyard with the key.

Paton had been butler at the castle for all of Serena's life, and she didn't seriously imagine he could be in league with this set of smugglers, nor that he wouldn't have reported any theft of his key. But it did seem extremely suspicious that his key had vanished just when the strangers appeared to have acquired one.

Jem was waiting for her in the old courtyard, carrying a lantern already lit. His large presence was something of a comfort as she unlocked the door, though her heart still beat like a rabbit's, and every hair on her neck seemed to stand up in expectation of some attack.

She threw the door wide.

Nothing happened.

The cellar was dark and quiet. As it should have been.

By the light of the lantern, they descended the old, worn stone steps. At first glance, the cellar looked as it always did, as Paton and Braithwaite between them kept it. Serena began to think she'd dreamed the delivery the night after her arrival, although she'd definitely been awake when she'd chased the stranger into the wood and faced his dagger.

Shivering, she began to walk around, past the rows of bottles and the barrels of ale, all lined up, as far as she could tell, as they had been the last time she'd been here. Years ago.

"I should have brought Paton," she said ruefully. "He would have known."

"Known what?" Jem asked.

"If there's anything unusual here."

"Why would there be?"

"I heard something the other night." She glanced at him. "And I saw smugglers rolling barrels in here."

"No." Jem shook his head. "They leave it at the gate or down on the beach. Paton always knows. So do I since I do the lifting these days."

"Then you're down here quite a lot?" Serena said eagerly. "Is everything as it should be?"

"Yes, of course," he said, patiently accompanying her on her tour.

"There's nothing...wait, what is that under the stairs?" He held up the lantern to illuminate the deeper gloom beneath the stone staircase.

Serena went closer. Four barrels and several smaller casks stood there. "Are those usual?"

Slowly, Jem shook his head. "No. No, they shouldn't be there at all."

A door banged at the top of the stairs, making Serena jump. Jem swung around, staring at her in alarm.

"M'lady?" came the familiar voice of George the footman.

Serena closed her eyes in relief.

"Are you down there, m'lady?" George called.

"Yes, yes, I'm here," she replied. "What is it?"

"Mrs. Grant is here."

Serena looked blankly at Jem. "Who the devil is Mrs. Grant?"

"The vicar's wife," Jem murmured.

"Oh, of course, Mr. Hoag has left us. I suppose I'd better... Thank you, Jem. Um...best say nothing of these barrels for now, but if you know of any intruders, if anyone knows... Oh dear, I feel people should be on their guard, but I don't want to alert whoever stole Paton's key. I'll think what's best, but for now, I'd better go and welcome the vicar's wife!"

Hurrying back to the main part of the castle, Serena brushed the cellar dust off her woolen gown.

"Mrs. Grant is in the drawing room, my lady," Paton told her as she crossed the front hall to the staircase.

"Thank you, Paton."

It was only when she walked into the drawing room and saw Lady Crowmore by the window, that she remembered the gossip. Wicked Kate Crowmore had married a mere country vicar.

"Yes, it is I," the lady said sardonically. "In fact, I married a curate, but he got swift promotion shortly afterward, thanks to your brother. How do you do, Serena?"

Remembering her manners, Serena went forward to shake hands. "I am well, just surprised. For some reason I never connected you with our new vicar! Braithwaite might have said. I'm very glad to see you."

"Are you as bored as all that?" the new Mrs. Grant said sympathetically.

Serena couldn't help giggling. "Actually, I'm not bored in the slightest." She rang the bell and told George, who entered immediately, to order tea and cakes.

"I heard you were in disgrace," Mrs. Grant said bluntly when the door closed. "It is something I am used to, so I have called with sympathy. Do you mind very much? About Sir Arthur, I mean."

"No, actually, though I suppose I wouldn't like that to get back to him."

Mrs. Grant peered at her. "You are a kindhearted girl, aren't you? We never had much to do with each other before. You were too young, and I wasn't respectable enough for us to mix together."

Serena laughed. "And now our roles are reversed! You look well as the vicar's wife."

"Thank you, I enjoy it," Mrs. Grant said surprisingly. "And if you want my opinion—though I can see no reason why you would—you wouldn't have enjoyed being Lady Maynard."

"He is very…staid," Serena allowed. "And I am not."

"All the same, flirting with Daxton is a dangerous game for anyone. Did you know he was married a few weeks ago? I met his wife. She is delightful."

"Yes, London is bursting with it," Serena said impatiently, more concerned with how Mrs. Grant had met the wife. Especially since the artist had seemed to know exactly who Daxton was. *Well, he's a fun person to be with. I'd probably flirt with him myself.* "He isn't here, is he?" she asked uneasily. "Dax?"

"No, they vanished into thin air. I believe they went to his estate at Daxton. Why?" She sat on the sofa, and when Serena sank down beside her, she said with surprising kindness. "You're not carrying a *tendre* for him, are you?"

Serena gave a slightly lopsided smile. "No. He's a lot more entertaining than Sir Arthur, but I knew he was only flirting. So was I. I'm afraid I was bored being good, but I'd honestly forgotten about the first dance when I stood up with him for the third."

"And so Sir Arthur got on his high horse, you broke the engagement, and Lady Braithwaite sent you up here in disgrace."

"Something like that," Serena admitted.

"Well, London's loss is our gain. The Assembly balls are still in full swing this month, so if you'd like to go this week, you must come with Tristram and me. I have an extra voucher."

"Oh, that would be lovely," she said wistfully. "I suppose Catherine Winslow will be there, and Bernard Muir, all my old friends. And I would meet your husband."

"You would," Mrs. Grant said gravely.

Serena was very tempted to keep her constrictions quiet and accept. She sighed. "I'm confined to barracks," she said humorously. "I'm not even meant to receive visitors or go into the garden without a chaperone."

"Well, you've broken both of those, haven't you?"

"How did you know?"

"Because I would have." Mrs. Grant regarded her thoughtfully. "What if I write to your mother, pleading your cause and offering to chaperone you to a few unexceptional events?"

"Could she reply in time?" Serena asked doubtfully.

"Sadly, no," Mrs. Grant mourned.

Serena cast her a speculative look. "You mean you are prepared to take the chance?"

"That she'll agree? Of course, she will. You are riper for mischief shut up here than going about and mixing with people. I should know. I'm only surprised you haven't got into trouble already."

Serena smiled, thinking of the artist and the dagger-wielding smuggler. "What trouble could one possibly get up to here?"

Chapter Four

A S SHE'D PLANNED with Mrs. Grant, Serena was driven the short distance into Blackhaven in the carriage the following day, accompanied by Miss Grey and Alice, who needed a new bonnet.

In the end, she'd said nothing to the rest of the household about the strange barrels, although she did tell Paton she'd glimpsed strangers in the grounds and that he should personally make sure the house was secure at night. She wasn't sure he took her terribly seriously, she didn't know what else she could do at this point. She comforted herself with the fact that no one else had been threatened. Her own experience would never have happened if she hadn't pursued the villain.

So, she let her mind dwell on more frivolous matters, like the Assembly ball, and the possibility of seeing, even encountering, the artist in town. She wished she knew his name. At least, since this was her first visit to Blackhaven since the spring, she had an excuse for gazing out of the window at everything and everyone and darting about the carriage for better views. But she didn't catch so much as a glimpse of his distinctive figure in the high street. He was probably in hiding from the bailiff.

The carriage dropped her at the vicarage and waited until she was admitted. She waved at Alice and Miss Grey and entered the domain of the lady once known as Wicked Kate.

In fact, Kate herself came bustling out of the kitchen at once and took her up to the bedchamber that would be hers for the night and duly admired the gold embroidered white ballgown she would wear for the evening.

"Let's have tea," Kate suggested, "and then we'll go and beard Tristram in the church. His christenings should be over by then."

"The house looks so different," Serena blurted. "So much brighter and yet more...comfortable."

"I like to think I have made it my own."

It was on the tip of her tongue to ask Kate why she had made such a peculiar and unfashionable marriage, but fortunately she managed to bite her tongue. And when they duly walked along the path to the church and met Mr. Grant, her question was answered.

He wasn't just the most handsome vicar she'd ever met, but would stand out as a handsome and distinguished man in any company. His manners were easy and friendly as he greeted her, not remotely obsequious or superior, and his few words exchanged with Kate were humorous. And Kate adored him. Not that she fawned upon him, but it stood out clearly in her eyes when she looked at him.

Serena was stunned.

Of course, she had encountered people content in their marriages before. Her sister Frances for one, and Gillie Muir for another. But they had both made advantageous, even brilliant matches. By the world's standards, Kate Crowmore's second marriage was beneath her. It served no duty to her family, brought her no wealth or position. And yet, she was happy.

It was a great deal of food for thought for Serena, who had gone so blithely into an engagement to the worthy man her family had approved over all her other suitors.

Emerging from the church, leaving Mr. Grant to go about his good works, the two ladies took a walk about the town until they came, inevitably, to the art gallery, where one could buy paintings of very mixed quality.

"Shall we go in?" Serena suggested. "I'm sure Gillie wrote to me that the paintings are much improved."

"I would say so," Kate agreed, pushing open the door. Inside, she was almost immediately besieged by two ladies quite unknown to

Serena, who was thus deprived of her opportunity to ask the questions that might lead to the identity of her own artist. She couldn't even tell which paintings in the gallery might be his since she didn't know his name, and had never seen his style.

He might, she reminded herself as she examined each picture in turn, be a terrible painter. It might explain why he had so little money that the bailiffs were after him. Some of the paintings were certainly terrible. Kate, who was an accomplished water colorist, was much better than some of the artists who exhibited here. Serena turned impulsively to tell her so, since she sensed a presence beside her, only she found herself gazing at a gentleman instead.

Her breath caught, because just for a moment, she thought it was her artist. But this man was slightly shorter and better dressed, and when he glanced down from his scrutiny of a landscape, she saw that in fact he was nothing like him. His lips were too thin, his eyes too flat, although a gleam of admiration did begin to sparkle as he bowed politely.

"Excuse me," she murmured, stepping around him.

In the end, it proved rather difficult to see all the pictures for both she and Kate both encountered old acquaintances who distracted them, and by the time they emerged from the gallery, Serena was no wiser about her artist. The only thing she knew for certain was that he hadn't been there when she had.

Their next call was to the smart new French modiste, Madame Monique. Kate wished to have a fitting for a new morning gown she was having made. While Kate and Madame vanished into the back of the shop, Serena admired the beautiful gauze muslins and silks and the fine gowns already made up and on display. It was a dangerous place to stay very long when one didn't wish to annoy one's parent by spending excessive amounts of money on gowns.

Which I'll never wear here in any case, she told herself. *Certainly not while I'm confined to barracks. I already have a trunk full of gowns I shan't wear for the foreseeable future.*

Eventually, she called out to Kate that she was going to the hat shop to see if Alice was still there, and dragged herself away from Madame Monique's creations. Not that the hat shop didn't provide temptations of its own, but at least if Alice was there, she could concentrate on her and make sure she bought nothing unbecoming.

From habit, she glanced in the coffee house window as she passed—and her heart gave a sudden dive. For there was her artist at a table with several other men who formed a comfortable, laughing group. Slouching back against the wall, he had one leg resting on a spare chair from the next table. He looked a perfect picture of idle decadence. And Serena had never seen anyone so carelessly yet so utterly attractive.

Before she could drag her gaze free, he glanced round and saw her. The smile just dying on his sensual lips, he held her gaze for an instant. She managed to nod before hastening across the street to the hat shop. Ridiculously, her heart hammered.

There was no sign of Alice or Miss Grey in the shop. Nor were there any other customers, but Mrs. Drake, the proprietor, was as delighted to see her as ever.

"I have only just had the pleasure of serving dear Lady Alice," she gushed. "Who chose exactly the right bonnet! I have to say I itched to find something for that nice Miss Grey, but I suppose she will not have the money or the time for such frivolities. Now, Lady Serena, are you looking for something in particular or would just like to look around for inspiration?"

A favorite game of Serena and Frances's had been to give each other characters, and then find hats to suit them. Mrs. Drake had indulged them, and it seemed she remembered, for she was quite happy to collect a fine selection of hats and leave them with Serena behind the screen, where her most favored customers could try her wares before the glass in greater privacy.

From the back of the shop, a baby cried.

"My granddaughter," Mrs. Drake said proudly. "I'm looking after her today while Harriet is in Carlisle. You will forgive me if I..."

"Of course," Serena said, "providing you let me see her before I go!

I shall be quite happy for now."

Removing her bonnet, Serena laid it on the chair and commenced randomly trying on hats—wide brimmed bonnets, frivolous little chip hats with gorgeous plumes, and mysteriously veiled confections with ornamental flowers.

In the back, the baby quieted for a few moments then set up a renewed bellowing. When the shop door opened and closed, Serena, tying a bonnet's silk ribbons under her chin, doubted Mrs. Drake heard it. At least her soothing voice did begin to comfort the crying child, reducing her to an occasional hiccup. If Serena hadn't known it would shock everyone, she would have offered to sit with the baby while Mrs. Drake served her new customer. Serena liked babies and was looking forward to being an aunt when Frances gave birth to her first child next month.

The footsteps in the shop paused. And abruptly, the artist's face appeared behind Serena's in the glass. Gasping, she tugged the bonnet ribbons tight in surprise and swung round to face him.

"What in the world are you doing in a ladies' hat shop?" she demanded.

His eyebrows rose. "Looking for you. I saw you from the coffee house and by the time I came out to speak to you, you'd vanished in here."

Clearly, he saw nothing odd or wrong in this. He truly was a free spirit, simply following his impulses. She should probably have been wary of the chaos he surely brought in his wake, but in fact, she found it curiously exciting.

"You've escaped," he remarked.

She frowned, trying to think for both of them while she plucked nervously at the ribbons. "I have. And you need to, before Mrs. Drake gets back. She doesn't like men in her shop, even husbands or fathers."

Ignoring that, he took a step nearer.

She warded him off with one hand. "Seriously, sir, we cannot talk here…"

"Where, then? You've knotted the ribbon. Let me."

To her astonishment, he raised both hands under her chin and began working on the knot. Her face and neck flamed under the light touch of his warm fingers. Although his attention was all given to his self-appointed task, and the brushing of his fingers against her skin was purely incidental, this did nothing to soothe her. No man had ever touched her so intimately before. She could smell the coffee on his breath, grew fascinated with the texture of his lips, which had already kissed hers. She felt oddly breathless and trembly. Most worrying of all, she had the insane urge to kiss him again.

In agitation, she caught at his wrist. "Stop, you mustn't...!"

"It's done." He let the ribbons fall through his fingers. "It doesn't suit you anyhow. Try this one."

He picked up a jaunty little red chip hat with two beautiful feathers, one curling down the side. Before she could snatch it from him, he placed it on her head and smiled into her eyes. Ignoring the tumbling sensation in her stomach, she scowled and pointed toward the door.

He threw up his hands in surrender and, still grinning, sauntered off. Serena wasn't sure if she was disappointed or relieved.

What just happened? She gazed at herself in the glass, somewhat numbly and began to smile.

He was right. The little red hat did suit her best.

Hastily, she snatched it off and crammed her own back on her head.

IT HAD BEEN a long time since Serena attended the local Assembly Room ball, and despite the far more glittering affairs she'd known in London, she looked forward to it with eagerness. Perhaps the fact that she was going against her mother and brother's stated wishes had something to do with her sense of excitement. Or the fact that she went chaperoned by someone as young, beautiful, and fashionable as Mrs. Grant. But mostly, although she knew it was unlikely in the extreme, she hoped her artist would be there.

Although he spoke like a gentleman and was clearly well-educated, he hardly looked as if he moved in polite society. And his bailiff troubles did not suggest a man who could afford a subscription to the ball—or even a single voucher. Still, as she entered with the Grants, she couldn't help looking around for his tall, dark figure. However, all the gentlemen she could see wore smart black coats and satin knee-breeches or well-fitting pantaloons. And they all had short, fashionable haircuts, not untidy mops. Clearly, this was not an event for a poor artist.

Still, the brief encounter in the hat shop, which can't have taken as much as a minute, had both shaken and further intrigued her. She would have liked to dance with him, flirt with him, in the safety of a chaperoned ball.

Besides, she couldn't help being curious as to what he'd wished to speak to her about. He must have discovered something about the smugglers.

But wishing for him would not bring him, and so, refusing to let his absence spoil her evening, she sat with the Grants and was delighted to renew her acquaintance with her old friend Catherine Winslow.

"I am finally to go to London for a season next year," Catherine confided. "Which frightens me half to death. I'm sure you'll be my only friend!"

"Actually, I doubt I'll be there," Serena said ruefully. "You must know I'm in disgrace since my engagement was broken."

"But you will make another match in no time," Catherine assured her. "You are so beautiful and lively."

"Lively is the problem," Serena explained. "One should be fashionably languid. As to another match, I'm not sure I want one. Which is probably fortunate since I am assured a broken engagement is disastrous in the marriage mart. No, we must make Gillie go to London for the season to keep you company, but you mustn't worry—I know you will 'take'!"

"It would be good," Catherine said, lowering her voice further, "but I'm hoping it won't matter too much. Don't say a word to anyone, but I have met a man who admires me."

Serena blinked at such modesty. "Cathy, lots of men admire you!"

"No, they don't. They're just used to me. The Comte is different."

"The Comte?" Serena pounced. "Tell me more."

"He is the Comte de Valère," Catherine said, blushing. "An émigré nobleman from France. I met him here at the Assembly ball earlier this month, and he danced with me twice. He has called on us three times since then, and taken me driving."

"Has he indeed? What is he like?"

"Oh, you shall see for yourself." Catherine gave a quick, excited smile. "He is coming tonight! I am promised to him for the waltz."

"I look forward to meeting him."

Serena stood up for the first dance of the evening with Mr. Grant, who proved to be an entertaining companion, and by the time they returned to Kate, she was surrounded by young men eager to be introduced to Serena for a dance, or to renew old acquaintance with her.

It was all very flattering for a girl who'd been told she was as good as ruined. But she remembered Kate's advice. "Never behave as though you have done anything wrong. Be seen, dance, laugh, have fun, but never beyond the line of what is pleasing, for there will be gossips here desperate to pass on any tiny transgression to their friends in London."

"I don't think I care if they do," Serena had observed.

"Your mother will care," Kate had warned. "And so will you, eventually. For your own sake, be a model of maidenly behavior. Until this nonsense blows over at least."

Serena could not easily discount Kate's advice, for the vicar's wife had had to deal with scandal of her own. Besides, she began to appreciate that Kate never actually judged her or anyone else. There was unexpected kindness in her.

For that reason, she decided to sit out the waltz, which was still considered to be fast in many circles. Instead, she took a stroll around the ballroom with her partner, Gillie's brother Bernard, catching up with his life and with news of his stepmother and tiny new brother. Apparently, he was as good as engaged to a Miss Smallwood, about whose beauty he waxed so lyrical that Serena's attention began to wander. To her indignation, she saw that Catherine sat still beside her mother, her head drooping in a disconsolate manner. The wretched émigré, clearly, had not turned up to claim his dance. Misleading someone as good natured and modest as Catherine—someone, moreover, so lacking in self-confidence—was unforgivably mean. *He'd better have a very good excuse,* she thought furiously, *or I shall give him the cut direct.*

She moved her gaze toward the nearby ballroom door, searching for Catherine's paragon among the new arrivals. And there, straight in front of her, stood the artist she so foolishly thought of as hers.

Gone was the long overcoat and the satchel, and he may have dragged a comb through his hair, but beside the other gentlemen with him, his plain black coat and breeches still looked unmistakably threadbare.

However, those around him didn't appear to notice. They were laughing at something he said, and he, smiling, bowed over the hand of a beautiful woman Serena did not know. Jealousy twisted through her, shocking her. Then he strolled away, just in time to seize a glass of champagne from a passing waiter. Raising the glass to drink, he looked about him. Serena was trying to drag her fascinated gaze free, when it finally clashed with his.

His eyebrows shot up. The glass lowered again, a smile blazing across his face as he walked directly toward her.

Serena, suddenly breathless with excitement, turned hastily back to Bernard, who, apparently catching sight of the artist, actually swerved toward him.

"Do you know him?" Serena demanded.

"Of course I do," Bernard replied. "Everyone does."

By this time, the artist was upon them, bowing with surprising grace. "Muir," he said, while offering his hand to Serena. She took it, since it would have been rude not to. "I've come to steal away your partner, who is far too beautiful not to be dancing."

"Lady Serena don't care to waltz," Bernard said indignantly, as though his honor had been impugned. "Wait for the next dance."

"Actually, my card is full," Serena declared, since they seemed to imagine they could decide such matters without her.

"You see?" the artist exclaimed. "Take pity on me, old chap. Half a dance is better than none."

Bernard threw up his hands. "Lady Serena must decide that one."

"Come," the artist said. Somehow, he still retained her gloved hand. His fingers were warm, insistent through the fine silk. "What harm could half a waltz do you? Everyone will know you do it from mere pity."

"I have no reason to pity you," she scoffed, and yet somehow, she was walking with him toward the dance floor.

"But you have, far more than you know. So tell me," he added before she could ask for clarification, "since we didn't have time in the milliner's. How *did* you escape your confinement?"

His arm encircled her waist, whirling her into the dance with rather more enthusiasm than was strictly proper.

"Mrs. Grant," she managed, "who is an old friend of my family's, offered to chaperone me."

"I'm very glad she did, for I missed you."

She lifted one eyebrow.

"I went to the orchard this morning and you weren't there."

"Should I have been?" she asked carelessly.

"Well, I hoped you would be. I wanted to tell you, a cargo was landed at Braithwaite Cove, one the usual gentlemen were not aware of, and one that certainly hasn't been distributed locally."

"It's in our cellar," Serena told him. "Jem and I found four barrels and some smaller casks that shouldn't have been there."

"Who is Jem?"

"One of our gardeners. I've known him forever and we can trust him implicitly. On the other hand…" She trailed off, frowning.

His thumb stroked her hand, presumably to draw her back to the conversation, although in fact, it distracted her further.

"On the other hand, what?" he prompted.

She drew in a breath, as if that could make her think again. "Paton, our butler, has lost his key to the cellar. I think someone must have stolen it and given it to the smugglers, which is not comfortable."

"No," he agreed, frowning. "No, it isn't, at all. Perhaps you could stay longer with the Grants?"

"And leave everyone else? No, I have to find out who's doing this, and make them take the barrels away. Or better still, we should remove the barrels from the castle, and then report them to the excisemen."

"The castle is a safe store for them," the artist mused, "because no one around here, including you, is prepared to land the earl in trouble by revealing the barrels' existence. They must be planning to take them somewhere else, further inland, probably."

"Then why not just take them right away?" Serena argued. "Why leave them here at all, if they should be elsewhere?"

"Because the time isn't right? Because they're waiting for someone or something, some signal that it's safe, perhaps."

"Perhaps," she agreed. He turned her a little too fast, reminding her just how close to him she stood. She was only too aware of the movement of his warm, lean body, of his strong arm at her back. She could smell him, sandalwood and something fresher and more elusive that she associated with the orchard, with woodland.

"Why are you here?" she blurted.

"You mean at the ball when I have no money? I sold a painting last month and bought a subscription."

"Why?"

"I wanted to paint Lady Arabella Niven and thought I'd find her here."

"Did you?"

"Find her or paint her?"

"Either!"

"Both," he said tranquilly. "In fact, if Alban would only pay me for the latter, I could get the bailiff off my back for a month or two."

"I expect Lady Arabella was one of the women you wanted to kiss as well as paint."

Instead of denying it, he appeared, infuriatingly, to consider it. "I wouldn't have minded, but by the time I met her, she only ever looked at Alban. It's not much fun kissing someone who's thinking of another man."

Serena regarded him with disfavor. "I think, sir, that you are an incorrigible flirt."

"Not really. I just like faces and I speak the truth. But I like flirting with you."

"You are *not* flirting with me," she said firmly, as though speaking the words made them true. "How do you manage to move in such elevated circles?"

"I often ask myself the same question. Bare-faced effrontery, I suppose. How else would I get to dance with you?"

"Why on earth do you *want* to dance with me?" she demanded, unwarily.

"Because I've wanted to hold you in my arms again ever since I kissed you."

Embarrassment flamed through her. At least, she thought it was embarrassment. To hide it, she glared at him. "*Will* you stop that?" If she hadn't been dancing, she'd have stamped her foot.

"Why?" he asked, depriving her of breath all over again.

"Oh, you're impossible. I'd storm off, if only it wouldn't cause even more talk!"

"Can't we just enjoy the waltz?"

In truth, it would have far too easy to relax into the dance, into his arms, surrounded only by music, as if there was no one else in the room.

"I don't even know your name," she said in frustration.

"I was hoping you didn't."

She blinked. "Why?"

"I don't know. I suppose I want you to like me as I am, without all the baggage that comes with names and worldly identities."

"Aha," she said wryly. "You are a royal prince travelling incognito."

"Would it help?" he asked.

"No," she said crossly.

"Then I'm not. I'm just what you think me, an artist without two pennies to rub together, who wants very badly to kiss you and paint you, and for once I don't know which I want more."

She tilted her chin. "Did you say that to Lady Arabella, too?"

As soon as the words were out, she regretted them. She had only meant to show him that she didn't take him seriously. Instead, she sounded appallingly jealous.

His gaze held hers when she tried to free it. "No." Again, his thumb moved in an apparently absent caress. "I wish we had longer. I wish things were different."

A frown twitched at her brow. Possibly for the first time in their odd acquaintance, she sensed he was serious. "What do you mean?"

His lips twisted. "I mean, I wish *I* were different," he said ruefully.

"I don't," she blurted.

She was too used to speaking her mind. And it was too difficult to keep pretending she didn't like his odd, intriguing company, just to salve her pride.

An arrested expression filled his eyes, swiftly followed by a look so warm it seemed to scorch her. A smile tugged at his lips. "Truly? I shall remember that when I see you from afar."

"Afar? You think I shall ignore you when I know your name? Stop being mysterious and tell me who you are."

But it was too late. The dance had ended, his arm slipped from her suddenly cold body, and etiquette demanded she curtsey to his bow.

"Come, I'll take you back to Kate," he said, offering his arm.

Mechanically, she laid her fingertips upon it. "So, you are upon first name terms with Kate," she noted. "*She* does not ignore you. And she is the vicar's wife!"

"Exactly."

"You are infuriating," she informed him as they arrived at Kate's chair.

"Thank you."

She didn't know if his gratitude was for the dance or the insult, for he merely bowed over her hand, cast a quick rueful smile at Kate and walked away.

"I see you've met Tamar," Kate said wryly.

Serena laughed. "Tamar," she crowed, loud enough for him to hear. He half-turned, casting a quick smile over his shoulder, but he didn't stop. "Tamar," she repeated with a quick frown. "Is he a *famous* painter?" she asked Kate, sitting next to her. "Is that where I've heard the name?"

"He's getting that way, in Blackhaven at least. Gillie might have mentioned him to you. But you're more likely to have heard of him as the impoverished marquis."

"*Lord* Tamar," she said blankly. "I thought he didn't exist. I thought the whole family vanished when the old marquis died in massive debt."

"Only into obscurity. Tamar came here because it was quieter than London or Brighton or Bath, but contained enough wealthy people to buy his paintings. He doesn't speak of his siblings, but I'm fairly sure he sends them most of what he earns."

"No wonder the bailiffs are after him."

Kate cast her a confused look. "Bailiffs can't touch him. As a peer, he can't be arrested for debt."

Serena frowned. "He said there was one haunting his doorstep."

"I expect it was a figure of speech. For *broke*."

Deliberately, Serena smoothed out her frown. "I expect it was. Someone owes him money."

"Perhaps it's time we bought a few paintings," Kate said neutrally.

"Perhaps it is… Where did he live before, then?"

"In the ruins of Tamar Abbey, according to Daxton. They all grew up there, he and his siblings, running wild, without any adult older than the new marquis who couldn't have been more than fifteen years old when he inherited."

"Why would he—" *Why would he think I'd hate him once I knew who he was?* Fortunately, she broke off before she asked the whole question aloud. It would have given away a greater friendship with him than she wanted Kate to be aware of.

Besides, she could probably answer it for herself. A low-born artist was beneath her. A marquis, however poor, was perfectly eligible by birth. Marrying a very wealthy heiress was his only hope of recovering his family's fortunes.

Serena was a wealthy heiress.

Fortune hunter... Lord Tamar was a fortune hunter. No wonder he flirted with her.

Chapter Five

SERENA HAD TO draw on all her London experience in order to appear to enjoy the rest of the ball. She danced, conversed, and laughed with such an apparently light heart that no one could have guessed the whirlpool of speculation, hurt, and indignation spinning in her head. And if she always knew where in the room Tamar was, if her gaze occasionally strayed toward him, it never lingered, and their eyes never met.

She knew whom he danced with, and that he took supper with the same beauty she'd seen him with earlier. But he never came near her, even during the second waltz.

It doesn't matter, she told herself. *It never mattered, it never will.*

Although she no longer knew whether or not she wanted him to pursue her, she was distinctly piqued that he didn't. Was this part of some plan she was too naive to understand?

It was only as they left the ball—a little early since both the Grants had to make an early start the following morning—that she saw him. She and Kate had just retrieved their wraps and emerged from the cloakroom to discover him at the front door with Kate's husband.

His expression was amiable but far too controlled for the carefree artist she thought she knew a little. Grant laughed at something he said, and then, seeing the ladies approach, stepped outside into the street, leaving Tamar to hold the door, in the absence of the usual Assembly Rooms doorman.

Tamar bowed them through with amusing exaggeration.

"I thank you, my lord," Kate said in the same spirit as she sailed through.

"Good night," Serena managed, moving after her. But at the last minute, just as she stood beside him in the doorway, desperation swamped her and she halted, turning impulsively toward him. "Are you?" she demanded.

The words *fortune hunter* hung between them. Neither pretended not to understand. *Are you a fortune hunter? Are you hunting mine?*

He said, "I'm walking away."

Her breath caught in hope, though of what she didn't know.

An unhappy smile tugged at his lips. "But you'll never be sure, now, will you, Serena?" A swift glance into the empty foyer, then he picked up her hand in both of his and pressed a strong, warm kiss to her knuckles. "Good night."

She opened her mouth to speak, but he dropped her hand as if it burned him.

"Serena?" Kate said from the street.

"She caught her shawl," Tamar said. "She's just coming."

And she was outside in the chill of the autumn night, walking blindly between Mr. and Mrs. Grant. She'd never felt so alone.

THE FOLLOWING MORNING, Tamar woke with a pounding in his head that wasn't all on the inside. Raising his head groggily from the sofa where he'd fallen asleep dead drunk in the small hours of the morning, he realized someone was knocking—nay, battering—at the door.

His friends all knew to call out to him. No one did.

"Bloody bum-bailiff," he muttered, and pulled the covers over his ears to go back to sleep. However, thirst drove him to the water jug which he poured directly down his throat before tearing off his shirt and pouring the rest over his head and shoulders.

He didn't want to go outside to work as long as Rivers haunted his doorstep, so, keeping the curtains shut, he set up the easel with the portrait of the wealthy mill owner. He even dabbed at it for a little before throwing down his brush in frustration. He couldn't settle to anything. His head was full of Serena, as he had last seen her, laughing and dancing with him; and Serena as he wanted her to be, making love, her beautiful, lush little body writhing with pleasure beneath him.

This was ridiculous. He should not be so obsessed. He'd done the right thing and walked away before he hurt her. Now he had to live with the decision, expel her from his mind...or at least concentrate on what the devil was going on at the castle. Without her knowing, he would still look out for her. In fact, he would have gone up this morning if he hadn't slept for so long that he'd failed to avoid Rivers. Now it would be evening, probably, before he could dodge past the bum.

Sighing, he looked restlessly around for something to do that wouldn't require too much attention.

Send Daxton his wedding present.

He'd finished the portrait of Dax and Lady Dax last week, but as usual, kept it aside for adjustments. Well, today, it would either be adjusted or sent on its way. If he could find it.

Fifteen minutes later, he stood back, scratching his head. The portrait was gone. Along with the few other pictures he'd failed to find the other day. This had gone beyond strange. Surely no one would steal his paintings...

But he began to think that had to be what was actually happening. And he wouldn't allow it, not Dax's portrait. That was a wedding gift and it had been promised. He could paint another, of course, but it wouldn't be the same, it wouldn't show them in the moment he wanted, the moment that was important to Dax *and* to Tamar.

He'd actually shrugged himself into his coat and was reaching for the door latch when he remembered about bloody Rivers. If he let justice take its course, what was left of the house and estate would collapse. Christianne would look after Anna, but her husband was not a wealthy man. She wouldn't let Julian or Sylvester leech off him. They'd go straight to the devil.

Besides which, he'd never discover what was happening to his paintings. Serena's sweet face swam into his mind's eye, as he'd seen her last night at the ball, her face lighting up with pleasure because she'd seen him. His stomach twisted with pain and a fury he hadn't known since he was fifteen years old and realized it was futile. His vile, stupid father had spoiled everything for anyone who had depended on him, and left his eldest son without the means to make any of it right. And so, Tamar had learned to live with it, with anything. It should be easy to bear the loss of Serena, someone he'd never even had. In time, it *would* be easy. He wouldn't sink with this either.

Instead, he strode to the back of the cottage. He was too big to wriggle out of the little window, so he opened it and yelled some nonsense. Smuggler Jack's wife, hanging washing outside her own cottage further along the row, stared over at him in consternation. Tamar waved and grinned, but by then, he'd heard the footsteps scraping along the path at the side of his studio.

Slamming the window shut and locked, he bolted to the front door, grabbing his satchel on the way. He leapt outside, pulling the door after him and locked it before sprinting along the road to the harbor. A couple of the fishermen along the row had come out of their cottages to cheer him on, so he gave them a quick salute in passing. Before he turned the corner, he heard Rivers yelling after him to stop. He grinned.

DAVIDSON, THE OWNER of the gallery, seemed pleased to see him. At this hour, the shop was quiet. Only one elderly lady and her small pug dog were perusing the pictures. Davidson, clearly suspecting the pug of malicious intent, kept a weather eye on it in case it lifted its leg. But he spared Tamar a grin and a greeting.

"Did you bring me another painting?"

"Not yet. I gave you four the other day."

"You should give me more while things are going so well. You must be really pleased with the price you got for the blue harbor scene."

Tamar paused in mid-stride. "But I never brought you the blue harbor."

"No, your assistant did, told me the price you'd decided on. I must admit I thought it was a mistake and argued against it, but you were right. You got every penny. I was thinking we could charge the same for any new works—"

"Wait a minute." Tamar rubbed his head, wishing he hadn't drunk so much last night. "I don't have an assistant."

Davidson blanched. "Of course you do," he said weakly. "You must have forgotten."

Tamar stared at him. "Is that something I'm likely to forget? I can't feed myself—how do you imagine I pay an assistant?"

"But it was definitely your painting, sir, the style was unmistakable. And I gave him the money only yesterday."

Tamar sank onto the comfortable chair intended for customers who were buying. "Why didn't you mention this when I was in before?"

Davidson shrugged. "When you didn't mention him, I assumed you'd dismissed him. Then he came in to collect the money and I thought he was still working for you after all. I thought it was a good thing…"

"Has he brought you anything else?" Tamar scoured the walls, searching for his own works.

"No," Davidson said nervously. "But he said he would jolly you along and bring more very soon."

Tamar scowled. "Well if you so much as catch sight of him again—anywhere—send me word immediately."

"Of course, but—"

"Did he have a name, this assistant? What did he look like?"

"Tall, dark-haired, gentlemanly… he said his name was Sylvester. Mr. Sylvester."

"*What?*" Tamar jerked his head around, staring at Davidson.

"You're sure it was Sylvester?"

"You know it isn't easy to trick me, my lord," Davidson said earnestly, "but this Sylvester seemed to know you so well—"

"I'll bet he did," Tamar said under his breath.

SERENA HAD ARRANGED for the carriage to call for her at three o'clock, but it seemed she might be a little late, for Kate talked her into riding with her over to Henrit to call on the Winslows. Kate, who was relatively wealthy in her own right, kept three horses at the local livery stables.

"I hear Catherine has an admirer," Serena said as they slowed their mounts to climb the hill to the Winslows' estate. "Though I gather he let her down last night."

"Ah yes, the Comte de Valère. I'd be interested to know what you think of him."

Serena raised her brows. She wasn't used to her opinion being sought.

Kate laughed. "Don't look at me like that, Serena. I know you're more than a pretty face."

"Why thank you." Serena gave an exaggerated bow. "At the moment, I think very little of him, but then, I've never met him. What is your opinion?"

"Oh, that like so many, he is charming, apparently well-travelled, and well-mannered. But he appeared suddenly in Blackhaven for his health, and I can see nothing wrong with him. If it wasn't that he's picked on Catherine, who is no heiress to speak of, I would suspect him of fortune hunting."

"Then he may genuinely care for her? She is, after all, a loveable girl."

"She is," Kate agreed. "Perhaps we should have tea at the hotel when we return and see if he makes an appearance."

However, as it happened, they didn't need to wait so long. The

Comte de Valère was discovered already taking tea with the Wins-lows. Listening with deference to Mr. Winslow, he stood at once when Serena and Kate were announced. He proved to be a distinguished, well-looking man of medium height and impeccable manners, with just a hint of French sophistication. Serena could see the attraction.

"Lady Serena," he greeted her upon introduction, bowing over her hand. "Then you are the Earl's sister and you live in that wonderful castle!"

"Yes, I am, and I do," she replied.

"I have only vague recollections of my own family's castle in France," he said. "I was very young when we left. But perhaps it is a good thing. I no longer take castles for granted but have learned to appreciate them."

Serena laughed. "Well, one doesn't appreciate them in the winter when they're wretchedly draughty and never get truly warm. Which is why we live mostly in the more modern house built on to it in the last century."

She moved on to speak to Catherine, who was looking flushed and happy. They sat together on the sofa, and under cover of the general conversation around them, Serena murmured, "Well? What is his excuse?"

"He was ill," Catherine said ecstatically. "Vilely. Unable to leave his bedchamber. But as you see, this was his first call this morning."

Although Serena thought he looked remarkably well for a man so sick less than twenty-four hours ago, she reserved judgment.

"What do your parents think of him?" she asked curiously.

"Oh, they like him well enough, but they would not like a match between us."

"Why not?"

Catherine sighed. "Because he is French, and because his family lost everything in the revolution. Neither of which is his fault."

Serena was obliged to agree. In fact, she had more than one reason to be grateful for the comte's presence, since it prevented their hostess from asking questions about her broken engagement and the reason for her exile to Blackhaven.

Mrs. Winslow had to content herself with observing, "Serena, you just missed Lord Daxton and his new bride."

"Yes, so Kate told me. I am eager to meet the new viscountess. I believe I know her cousin, Miss Shelby."

Fortunately, conversation then veered onto gossip about the Shelbys, and not long afterward, Serena suggested to Kate that they should get back in time to meet her carriage in Blackhaven. Rather to her surprise, the Comte de Valère left at the same time. Since he had also ridden, he escorted them back to town.

At last, Serena began to see what had captivated her friend. Away from the elder Winslows' formality, he proved to be witty and entertaining company, and she was almost sorry when they parted at the stables.

"Poor Catherine," Kate said ruefully.

"Why poor?" Serena asked in surprise. "I think I actually like him."

"Hence, poor Catherine. You eclipse her, you know."

Stricken, Serena gazed at her. "Surely not! I did not mean—"

"You did nothing to be ashamed of," Kate assured her. "As if he can be swayed away from her by you in an hour, then she is better off without him."

"Indubitably!"

RETURNING TO THE castle in time for tea with her sisters and Miss Grey, Serena entertained everyone with descriptions of the ball and the supper, and duly admired Alice's new bonnet before showing them all the red chip hat with the feathers which she'd been unable to stop herself from buying.

"Yours is much prettier than mine," Alice said discontentedly.

"Oh, no, it's just different," Serena assured her. "And this one would be quite unsuitable for you until you're older. In fact, it's not terribly suitable for me in the present circumstances, so I have no real excuse for buying it."

After tea, they took a walk in the grounds, and to distract herself from thoughts of the artist, who kept popping into her head with annoying regularity, Serena focused her mind on the smugglers. It came to her that in order to be sure when the smugglers came back, she needed to hide in the cellar all night.

This was a somewhat daunting proposition, for as well as being cold and uncomfortable, she doubted she could stay awake all night. And then these smugglers were dangerous men. One had already pursued her with a knife. She really didn't want to be caught by him in the cellar, with nowhere to run and nobody to protect her.

But then, problems were only there to be solved. It would be dark and they would not expect anyone to be there. She was sure she could find a secure hiding place from where she could watch and listen and learn who they were and where they were taking their contraband. As for protecting herself... There was a long and heavy cast iron poker by the fire in her chamber. That would have to suffice.

All she had to do was obtain the cellar key once more.

When they returned to the castle and the others ran upstairs to change, Serena casually asked Paton for the key.

"Mrs. Gaskell keeps it now," he replied, with a sniff. Clearly, he was not happy with this arrangement, but recognized the fault as his for having lost his own key. It was inconvenient for Serena too, since Mrs. Gaskell was more likely to ask questions. Neither, of course, would allow her to spend the night in the cellar.

So, with only faint twinges of guilt for lying, Serena approached the housekeeper before dinner, clutching an old letter of her brother's in her hand.

"Mrs. Gaskell, may I have the cellar key again? I've just reread his lordship's letter and I got the name of the wine completely wrong. Now, I need to go and count the correct bottles."

She was aided by the fact that Mrs. Gaskell was in full flood scolding the kitchen maid at the time, and merely handed over the key with a frown of suppressed irritation. Serena hid it in her chamber for later.

If Mrs. Gaskell asked for it tonight, she'd promise to bring it to her later. The housekeeper would not harass her in her bedchamber for such a reason…she hoped.

THE LANDLORD OF the tavern was not fond of names. But since Tamar had discovered no Sylvester registered at the hotel, he was fairly sure his picture thief was staying at the seedier establishment frequented by sailors and villains of various sorts. Eventually, he received reluctant confirmation from the landlord when he described his suspect.

"You won't mind," Tamar said easily, "if I step upstairs and pay him a visit?"

"I will mind, because he isn't here," the landlord said bluntly. "He went out."

Tamar gazed thoughtfully at the landlord. He could go up and reclaim his money, if the thief was stupid enough to leave it unattended in this establishment. Which he doubted.

"Where did he go?" Tamar asked.

The landlord shrugged. "Miss Pinkie's, probably."

The brothel? With my money? He rather liked the idea of going round there and thrashing the little bastard while his pants were down.

On the other hand, "Sylvester" could wait. It was more important that Serena remained safe. So, he left his hair-of-the-dog only half-finished and returned warily to his studio, where he left his satchel and instead, pocketed his father's old pistol and the tinder box. Then, swiping up a lantern, he went to Jack's and offered a penny to his son for crawling in the back window and bolting the door from the inside.

It left the window unlocked, of course, but no grown man could get in that way anyhow. After carefully examining the lock, he'd come to the conclusion it had been simply been picked. It wasn't so easy to unbolt the door from the other side.

That done, he walked swiftly up to the castle, and, avoiding the locked gates, took his usual route into the grounds—under the bottom hedge. The hole was harder to find in the dark and he was forced to light the lantern. He muted the light by covering it with his neck cloth as he drew nearer the castle building, then blowing it out altogether.

He could only see a couple of faint lights at the front of the house, which looked shut up for the night. He moved round the side to the old courtyard, where the cellar was, and where Serena had seen the smugglers. All appeared quiet there, too, so he walked under the arch and up the sloping grass to the stone wall from where he could look down on the yard. Moving along it, he found shelter from the spitting rain under a crooked tree, where he sat down, his back against the trunk, and prepared to watch and wait.

Which was a dull way to spend one's time. He amused himself by planning a painting of the castle by night, with just that faintest of lights at one window. He wondered who slept there—servants, probably, or perhaps the governess.

Despite his best of intentions, he had almost nodded off when a scraping sound in the yard below made him sit bolt-upright, peering into the darkness. It was wood scraping against stone, and the cellar door was moving open, very slowly.

Tamar's skin prickled. Christ, they'd been inside all the time, and now they were coming out. Soundlessly, he pulled himself to his feet and closed his fingers around the cold pistol in his pocket. It wasn't loaded but he could at least threaten with it if necessary. If he remained hidden, he could watch and follow and discover where they were taking the contraband. Whatever it was.

A pale hand holding a night candle slowly emerged from the half-open cellar door. It didn't move and neither did its owner. Above, Tamar stood equally still, poised to act one way or another.

Candle and hand withdrew, and the door began to close again.

Tamar scowled. What was going on here? Was someone checking the way was clear, preparatory to removing the barrels? It seemed the likeliest solution, so he waited, straining his ears for sounds of movement. You couldn't shift a heavy barrel over stone without making some noise, but Tamar heard none.

Making his decision, he vaulted over the wall and dropped into the yard. He waited, half crouching, to see if his soft thud had been heard inside. Hearing nothing, he loped forward to the door and tried it gingerly. It moved silently on well-oiled hinges.

Inside, it wasn't pitch dark. A candle at the foot of a worn stone staircase dimly showed him the way. He took the pistol from his pocket and crept down, every sense on high alert, for he'd no idea if the candle was designed to lure him in, or if it had just been forgotten about.

As he reached the bottom of the stairs, he turned to pick up the candle, and something whooshed toward him from the left. He spun around, his fist already pulled back to strike, and the rushing creature slid to a halt only inches from him.

A pale figure in a long, white gown, ghostly in the candlelight, stared up at him. She held a cast-iron poker in one hand, ready to strike.

"Serena?" he said in disbelief, unfurling his fist and dropping it to his side.

The poker clattered to the stone floor. "You?" she all but sobbed and hurled her trembling body against his.

Chapter Six

SERENA, HAVING WORKED up the courage to fly at the armed intruder, whom she'd seen only in shadow and silhouette as he'd crept down the stairs, collapsed on Tamar's chest in utter relief.

After a stunned instant, his arms wrapped around her, strong and warm and comforting. Something touched her hair—his chin, perhaps, or his lips.

"There," he murmured. "I have you. I have you." He stroked her hair once, then drew her head back. "Serena, are you alone here? Was that you who opened the cellar door?"

"Yes, I wanted to see if anything was moving outside, and then I thought I heard something. Someone breathing."

"Me, probably," he said ruefully. "It never entered my head it would be you creeping about in the middle of the night."

"At least I live here," she retorted.

"Fair point," he allowed. "Only why didn't you lock the cellar door behind you? So you could hit me with that very lethal looking poker?"

"No, it doesn't lock from the inside. I was going to hide, only you followed me too quickly and I was still in the middle of the cellar when I saw you coming down. I thought I might be able to knock you out with the poker."

"Optimistic," he observed.

"And *then*," she continued, scowling, "tie you up before you came round. Then Jem could make you tell us everything."

He peered over her head into the darkness again. "Is Jem here, too?"

"Oh no. I meant to speak to him in the morning."

Now that she was no longer frightened, she began to realize how little she was wearing—nothing but her night rail—and how sinfully delicious it felt to be held so close to him. Her body seemed to be singing and purring for more at the same time.

"Well, it was a good plan," he said generously, "though I'm not sorry to have escaped the poker. Only, perhaps the next time you go setting traps for armed smugglers, you should wear more than your nightgown and bring a few armed, preferably large, male friends."

She shoved at his chest. "You're laughing at me."

He smiled. "No, I'm still delighting in you."

Although his arms had loosened a little, she hadn't pulled free. She was alone with him in the semi-darkness, wearing hardly anything and she found it difficult to breathe.

She tilted her chin. "I thought you'd walked away."

"I have. I can still delight. And protect."

She licked her dry lips. He followed the movement with a peculiar hunger that made her stomach squirm. Despite the chill of the cellar, heat surged through her.

She swallowed. "Is it necessary to hold me quite so close in order to do so?"

"It helps," he said huskily. "With the delight. Not so much with protection." His hand was in her hair again, tilting up her face as he lowered his. His lips parted, and her stomach dived in anticipation. "Christ, you're beautiful," he whispered.

She melted, her eyes closing as his fingers fisted in her hair and his breath caressed her lips. And then he stilled. His breath was too quick, too shallow.

His hands fell away. "Serena, I can't do this to you," he said in anguish, stumbling back from her into the side of the staircase.

From sheer need, she followed. Rising on tiptoe, she seized his face between her hands and kissed him full on the mouth. Only then did fear swamp her, fear of what she'd done, fear of rejection. Of acceptance. He stared at her, breathing hard.

Then he seized her in his arms, hauling her against him. "One kiss," he muttered, "just one more."

And then her mouth was crushed beneath his in the kind of wild, devouring kiss she'd never imagined. At once rough and tender, it overwhelmed her, battering her with sensation and desires she barely understood. He held her nape, caressing, keeping her head in the position he wanted as he plundered her mouth.

With a sound like a sob, she threw her arms around his neck, and his grip tightened, grinding her hips and breasts into his hard body. She felt the shock of his erection against her abdomen, though it thrilled rather than appalled her.

He'd said one kiss, but it seemed it would never stop. She never wanted it to stop, even when his hands swept over her body, caressing her breasts and waist and hips and slid over her bottom.

Trembling and eager, she rejoiced in the storm she'd provoked, kissing him back with blind, instinctive passion. He seemed to like it, for he groaned, opening his mouth wider before he broke the kiss and dragged his lips across her jaw to her neck, where he paused, panting.

His heart pounded against her.

Very slowly, he lifted his head and stepped back. "You don't even know, do you? What you do to me? What I wish to do to you…"

She swallowed. "I understand it more than I understand you walking away. If you like me."

He laughed softly, deep in his throat. "*If?* Dear God…"

"You are a marquis, I am an earl's daughter. It's not even unsuitable."

"You are possessed of a fortune. I'm possessed of a mountain of debt and three, if not four, dependent and expensive siblings. *That* is unsuitable. I will not hunt your fortune, Serena. Not yours."

"The entire marriage mart is a fortune hunt," she said impatiently. "Do you imagine Sir Arthur asked for my hand from undying love? Or that I accepted it for any reason other than settlements, position, and alliance with his family?"

"I can bring you none of these things."

"I *want* none of them." It was true. She'd just never allowed herself to acknowledge it before.

He dragged one hand through his hair. "Serena, *no one* wants alliance with my family. Except perhaps some filthy-rich cit who wants a title for his underbred daughter. God help her."

She searched his eyes, frowning, desperate, the thrill of his recent embrace still tingling through her. "Then you *are* a fortune hunter? You just need a bigger fortune than mine."

He closed his eyes. "I need a bigger fortune than yours."

But she'd already seen the truth. "You're lying," she crowed. "Perhaps not about what you need, but certainly about what you want."

His eyes gleamed. "If you challenge me again, I'll take you on the cellar floor."

Desire coursed through her. "No, you won't," she said unsteadily. "You're a gentleman, Lord Tamar."

He gave a twisted smile. "By my own lights at least. I doubt your brother would agree with you if he'd seen me manhandling you a moment ago. And I couldn't blame him. Did I hurt you?"

She shook her head. But in truth, she didn't know. Those moments in his arms had shattered her, both emotionally and physically. She suspected she could now be hurt a great deal more. She understood she was playing with fire. And yet, nothing in the world had ever been so exciting, so *important.*

He said unsteadily, "You must be freezing."

She was certainly shaking, though she didn't know if it was from the cold or from his presence.

"I have a blanket," she said, suddenly embarrassed by her immodest appearance, although considering his recent caresses, there wasn't much he didn't already know. Nevertheless, she turned from him, hurrying across the cellar to the little camp she'd made in the far corner, behind the large barrels of ale.

Seizing up the blanket, she swung it around her shoulders like armor.

But he'd followed her, with the candle, seen her little makeshift bed. "You were sleeping here," he uttered, clearly appalled.

"Well, they'd never have seen me," she said defensively. "And I might have learned something, if they'd only come tonight. Their barrels are over there." She pointed under the stairs, and after another moment frowning at her, apparently speechless, he swung around and strode back across the floor to the foreign barrels. She followed more slowly, hugging the blanket around her.

"These ones?" he said, slapping the side of one.

"Yes, but here's the thing. They've been here. They must have come last night when I was at Kate's, for there are two less barrels than before."

"Then at least they're moving them," he said uneasily, "although they could come back at any time." He gave the large barrel a push, wobbling it on the floor. "You know, this feels wrong."

He delved into the capacious pocket of his coat and retrieved a penknife, with which he began to work off the top of the barrel.

"Won't they notice?" she asked uneasily.

"I can't see that it matters. They just need to get them to wherever they're needed. And they know we won't tell the authorities for fear of implicating your family."

He pried off the lid, which fell on the floor.

She stepped closer. "Brandy?" she hazarded. "Or wine?"

"Neither," he said slowly, dipping one finger inside.

By the light of the candle, she peered in at what looked like white powder. "What on earth...?"

Tamar sniffed the grains on his finger, then touched them with his tongue, before raising his eyes to hers. "Gunpowder."

"*Gunpowder?*" Serena moved closer until she stood beside him, staring at the harmless looking contents. "Dear God, why would anyone store gunpowder in our cellar? Surely they can't mean to blow up the castle! Why would they do that? I know Braithwaite has recently gone into politics, but no one can hate him for that *yet*."

"In any case, they're taking it somewhere else," Tamar said, dragging his hand through his hair.

"Or they mean to destroy more than one place. How much damage would this amount of gunpowder do?"

"I don't know." Absently, Tamar picked up the lid of the barrel and began to fit it back on. "We can't talk about it here, and you certainly can't sleep here."

Under her slightly bemused gaze, he strode across the room and seized her pillow and the other blanket from the floor. The keys to the cellar and to the side door, which must have got tangled in the bedding, clattered to the floor. Serena hastened to retrieve them, then took up the candle and led the way upstairs and out into the courtyard. She locked the door while Tamar scanned the darkness for signs of anyone approaching or even watching. Apparently, he saw nothing out of the ordinary, for he followed her round to the side door without a word.

As she unlocked the side door, he said quietly, "We need to talk about this. We can't keep gunpowder to ourselves."

"I know." She sighed, then folded one arm quickly across her stomach to muffle it's ill-mannered rumbling. "Sorry, I'm starving, suddenly."

"Me, too."

She hesitated, then, opening the door wide, she said, "Come down to the kitchen. There's always something in the larder and no one will be there at this time of night."

"I can't," he said with flattering regret. "If I'm found there, you'll be ruined."

"Nonsense. I'll cast all the blame on Rosie the kitchen maid."

His breath caught on a laugh. "No, you won't."

"I won't need to. Kitchens are innocent, and you could be there for anyone. Unless you're discovered here by the door carrying my bedding."

He stepped inside with alacrity, and she closed the door and locked it before leading the way through the various darkened rooms toward the main entrance hall. In the final room, the library, she pointed at the shadowy sofa to signal he should leave her pillow and blanket there. Then, she tripped across the hall toward the back of the house, through the servants' door and downstairs to the kitchen.

There, it was cozy and warm, with heat still radiating from the stove. She lit two lamps from her candle and blew it out before walking to the larder in search of nourishment. Tamar, still silent, seemed to watch her every move, which was disconcerting as well as curiously arousing. Her whole body tingled when she remembered the heated embrace in the cellar.

"Cold chicken?" she suggested. "And there's most of a loaf and some fruit. Oh, and look, there's still chocolate cake! Cook makes the most delicious chocolate cake. We had it for tea." Aware she was babbling, she bit her lip, picking up the plates containing the chicken and the cake and turning.

Tamar stood right behind her. Her surprised gaze clashed with his heated one, but he only took the plates from her and walked away to lay them on the table. She followed with the bread and butter.

"Water or ale?" she asked prosaically.

"Water, if you please."

She set down two cups with the plates and sat at one end of the table. He sat in the chair on her right.

"Who do we tell?" she asked, before the gunpowder took second importance in her mind, well behind his presence. "Mr. Winslow, the magistrate? Or Major Doverton at the barracks?"

"Both, probably." He picked up the knife and hastily carved several slices of chicken. "But I shouldn't be involved, for your sake. I've no reason to be poking about your cellar."

"I'll get Paton to discover it, and then we can send word to every-one." She frowned, helping herself to the chicken he politely offered, and then reaching for the bread. "Only I still don't know who stole Paton's key."

"I've been thinking about that. It could have been anyone, not necessarily one of the servants here. He probably keeps it on a chain with his other keys and takes the whole lot with him to Blackhaven or Carlisle, or wherever else he goes."

"He does," she admitted. "I asked him. But it doesn't rule out our people either. After all, *someone* must have come up with the idea of using our cellar."

"We can worry about that later," Tamar said firmly. "The first thing we have to do is get the gunpowder away from here before it blows up the castle—whether or not anyone means it to."

She shivered. "I can't quarrel with that."

"I'll watch the door until first light," Tamar said. "And then you must get your servants to—" He broke off, hearing what she did, the soft shuffle of feet on the stairs.

In alarm, he scanned the kitchen for hiding places, but Serena touched his arm to make him stay. She'd already recognized the whispering voices. And then, Maria and Alice appeared at the foot of the stairs, wearing only their nightgowns and wrappers, and highly indignant expressions.

"Serena!" Alice exclaimed in outrage. "You're finishing the chocolate cake!"

"I knew you were up to something!" Maria said bitterly.

As one, their attention shifted from the cake to Lord Tamar, and their eyes widened.

"Serena?" Maria said, hurrying across to her, Alice trotting at her heels. "What...? Who is...?"

"This is Lord Tamar and he's perfectly safe," Serena said in as down-to-earth a manner as she could "He is helping me solve a mystery."

Alice looked quite relieved, although Maria remained unconvinced. "Yes, well, I'm fairly certain Mama will have a fit of the vapors if she finds out he's helping you in the kitchen at two o'clock in the morning."

"Which is why we mustn't tell her," Serena said. "Or anyone else for that matter, for I doubt they would understand either. Um, Lord Tamar, allow me to present my sisters, Lady Maria and Lady Alice."

Tamar half-stood to bow. "Very glad to make your acquaintance," he said, apparently accepting the situation in his stride. "Pull up a chair. Have some chocolate cake before your sister consumes it all."

It seemed to be just the right manner, for even Maria who, on the cusp of sixteen, was obsessed with matters of etiquette, didn't try to curtsey in her night rail. Instead, she commanded, "Spoons!" to Alice and threw herself into the chair on Serena's other side.

"Did you meet Lord Tamar at the ball last night?" Alice demanded, all but throwing a spoon at her sister in her hurry to get to the cake.

"Well, I saw him there," Serena admitted. "But we'd met before."

"In London?"

"No," Tamar said cheerfully. "Here at Braithwaite. I was trespassing in order to paint, and Lady Serena thought I was a new gardener."

"You do look a bit like a gardener," Alice allowed.

"That's because I've been crawling through earth and hedges to spy on your cellar."

"What's in the cellar?" Maria asked, clearly intrigued in spite of herself.

"Illicit brandy," Alice said scathingly.

"Gunpowder," Serena said, deciding honesty was best at this point.

Silence greeted her. The girls' mouths fell open.

Then a voice called from the top of the stairs. "Maria? Alice, are you there?"

"Miss Grey," Alice said in dismay. "Now we are in the basket."

"Nonsense," Serena said. The night had become so unreal that she was happy to see anyone. She raised her voice. "Have you come for chocolate cake, Miss Grey?"

"Oh yes!" That was Helen's voice rather than Miss Grey's, swiftly followed by an enthusiastic patter of feet on the stairs. Helen's small figure almost skidded into the chair beside Tamar, before the governess had even reached the foot of the stairs.

Tamar passed Helen what was left of the cake.

"Thank you," she beamed, halving the cake with his knife. "Um…who are you?"

"Tamar. Who are you?"

"Helen."

"And this is Miss Grey," Serena pronounced, "who is now sworn to secrecy."

Miss Grey, a large shawl over her nightgown, stood at the kitchen door, apparently stunned. "What are you all doing here at this hour?" she demanded.

"Cake," Helen said happily. "We saved you a piece."

Miss Grey straightened her shoulders. "I'm sorry. I cannot imagine that the countess, your mother, would countenance a nighttime feast in the kitchen with a strange man, even for Cook's chocolate cake."

"You're right," Serena agreed. "She wouldn't. But this is an emergency. I assure you it wasn't preplanned, or we would, of course, have included you."

Miss Grey emitted a sound that might have been choked back laughter. Serena smiled at her encouragingly.

"We heard a noise and came downstairs," Maria explained, "and then we followed the noise to the kitchen where we found Serena and Lord Tamar eating the cake."

"Naturally, you had to have your share," Miss Grey said dryly. "Well, your clattering in the passage woke Helen who thought there were intruders in the house and came to tell you, Maria, only you weren't in bed, so she woke me in panic."

"Please sit down, Miss Grey," Serena begged. "You might help us with our problem." She turned to Tamar. "Miss Grey is extremely clever."

"But not subject to flattery," the governess retorted. "And if I sit with you, it makes me complicit and more likely to keep this from your mother. Which I can't, Lady Serena."

"Not if she asks," Serena agreed. "That wouldn't be right. But Lord Tamar is here in all innocence to help us with a problem."

"What problem?" Miss Grey challenged at once. Clearly, she didn't believe a word of it.

"Gunpowder," Alice said, pulling out a chair for her. "In our cellar."

Miss Grey moved and sank into the chair, blinking at the small piece of cake that Helen shoved in front of her. "You had better tell me," she said with resignation.

Chapter Seven

A S WITH MOST situations in is life, Tamar simply enjoyed the moment. He knew he shouldn't have touched Serena, and yet he couldn't be sorry that he had. That she'd kissed him back, that she'd seemed to want him as some kind of formal suitor both stunned him and warmed him to the bottom of his heart. It could never be, of course, and she'd see that in time, but for now, it was unspeakably sweet, something to hug to himself in the cold light of reality.

Which, at the moment, was the bizarre discovery of gunpowder, and eating chocolate cake with some very young ladies and their governess.

To his surprise, the governess supported Serena in her veto of his idea that he should watch the cellar door from his old hiding place for the rest of the night.

"There must be somewhere from inside that gives one the same view," she said.

Tamar raised his brows. "I thought you'd be the first to push me out the door and lock it."

She met his gaze with very un-governess-like boldness. "Lady Serena appears to trust you, and I trust her judgment of character."

"Do you?" Serena said, apparently both surprised and touched. After all, to the world, she was the girl who'd ruined her engagement by dancing three times with Dax, a notorious rake of the first order. Not everyone would have recognized that Dax wouldn't hurt her, but Serena probably had. And perhaps, unconsciously, she'd wanted to end her dull but worthy engagement.

I would make her happy.

The wistful thought hit him from nowhere, causing his lips to twist in sheer self-mockery. *No, I wouldn't. I'd make her miserable, and poor, and the sparkle of her brilliant eyes would dull...* He couldn't bear that. At even the thought of it, pain clawed at his gut.

This was stupid. He'd known her for what, three days? Four? Ruthlessly, he squashed the pointless meanderings of his mind and refocused on the discussion in hand.

"My bedchamber looks onto the old courtyard," Serena said. "That was how I saw them in the first place."

"Well, Lord Tamar can hardly watch from there," Miss Grey pointed out.

Serena blushed adorably. "Of course not. But he could see from the rooms beneath just as easily. There's the still room and a spare bedchamber."

"It sounds more comfortable than the oak tree," Tamar admitted, glad of the table to hide his body's wayward reaction to the thought of Serena's bedchamber.

"We'll show you where it is," Lady Helen offered, springing to her feet.

"And then it's back to bed," Serena said, "for all of us! Except poor Lord Tamar, of course."

They all escorted him out of the kitchen and upstairs, then along winding passages to another, narrower staircase in an older part of the house.

"Serena prefers it here," Alice offered.

"Why is that?" Tamar asked.

"I think Frances and I were just desperate to grow up and get away from the nursery," Serena said, almost ruefully. She cast the governess a quick smile. "We never had a Miss Grey."

"No, you had a Miss George," Maria recalled with a shudder. "Terrifying woman. She retired from the position, thank God."

"I don't blame her," Miss Grey said tartly. "And I can see why you've run through so many governesses since then—you have no respect."

"We have for you," Helen said, hugging her arm.

Miss Grey snorted, and Serena cast a quick conspiratorial smile at Tamar that almost undid him. He wanted this girl as his friend. Mind you, there was something appealing about all of them, something about this bizarre expedition that reminded him of his own family just after the old marquis had died. A sense of freedom and fun...before it had all gone wrong and they'd all grown up for the worse.

He veered away from the memory as Maria threw open a door on the left of the wood-paneled passage. The bedchamber inside smelled a little musty from lack of use, but when he walked over to the window, it was clean enough to see clearly down onto the courtyard below. He might not have been able to see the cellar door, but he could see anyone entering the yard.

Serena said, "You don't have to do this, you know. I could watch."

"No, you must have been up half of last night," he protested.

"So must you."

He had, and it had not been a night well spent. Fortunately, the ill-effects were little more than a distant memory. A lot seemed to have happened since he'd woken up on his lumpy couch.

"I'm used to it," he said.

Despite the younger girls' offer to keep him company, Serena and Miss Grey herded them out and closed the door. He could hear their voices in lively discussion, fading as they walked away. The sound of Serena's infectious laugh was unmistakable.

His stomach twisted, but he refused to acknowledge regret or waste time on imagining what might have been. Instead, he folded himself onto the window seat and settled in to watch and listen.

As dawn broke, he doubted any strangers would risk venturing near the castle now. And it was time he left before he was seen by the servants.

Unwinding himself from the window seat, he stretched prodigiously and picked up his coat. Although he couldn't yet hear any movement in the castle, it would be bustling soon enough.

He walked to the door and opened it as softly as he could. A quick glance showed him the passage was empty, so he emerged, closed the door behind him, and walked along to the stairs—where he almost bumped into Serena.

"Oh," she gasped. "I was just coming to show you the way out."

Trapped between him and the step behind her, she stood much too close to him for her own good. He could have stepped aside, but he didn't want to. He could smell her subtle scent, like spring flowers and fresh sunny mornings after rain. Her chest rose and fell too quickly, as though she'd run down from her own chamber. Or was affected by his nearness. His arms ached to hold her again, to taste her willing lips. To take her back to the chamber he'd just left and show her delight.

Her tongue darted out, nervously wetting her lips. He swallowed. Forcing his heavy feet to move, he turned and led the way downstairs, only too aware of her every movement behind him.

"This way," she murmured, squeezing past him at the foot of the stairs. Her gown swished against his leg, her shoulder brushed his arm.

He followed her along the passage to the side-door they'd entered by last night. He watched her slender hand insert the key in the lock and turn it, and couldn't help remembering the touch of her soft fingertips on his cheek, his nape. There were so many places he wanted her to touch him.

Without conscious volition, he moved closer, just as she stepped back to open the door. He didn't care that she stood on his toes, for her rear bumped against him and the heat of her body, the scent of her skin, inflamed him.

She gasped, whisking herself away, and though he truly didn't mean to, his hand shot out, seizing her elbow and spinning her back against him.

He stared greedily down into her face, her parted, rosy lips and her beautiful, brilliant eyes, full of surprise and hope and trust.

It was the trust that saved her.

Emitting a sound between a groan and laughter, he released her.

"God help me," he said. "Open the door and throw me out."

Of course, he couldn't wait, and his hand closed over hers on the latch, lifting it and drawing the door open. Her hand twisted under his, as if it would be free. At once, he dropped his hand and slipped hastily around the door.

"Let me know what happens," he said huskily.

"We might take a walk in the orchard this afternoon," she murmured, and his gaze at once flew back to her. She wasn't angry. She wasn't angry at all.

He shouldn't have felt relieved. He shouldn't have been glad. But he was. He liked her.

Managing a faint upward quirk of his lips, he turned and strode away from the house. He broke into a run, trying to ease the ache of longing.

SERENA WAS SO impatient that first thing, she sent servants off with notes to both Mr. Winslow the magistrate and Major Doverton at the barracks. Although the notes explained that her butler had discovered strange barrels of gunpowder in the castle cellar, she hadn't yet had time to take Paton down there to look.

Paton, however, had known her a long time, and when she finally managed to drag him to the cellar and show him what she'd found, he expressed no surprise at her strange behavior, and accepted without a murmur his role of discoverer before the magistrate.

Mr. Winslow and the major arrived together, and scratched their heads over the barrels, which they agreed did indeed contain gunpowder.

"Perhaps your supplies have been robbed?" Mr. Winslow suggested to the major. "Either at the barracks or en route?"

Doverton shook his head. "I've heard of no such thing, and I don't have so much else to do that I don't keep track of all our supplies." Like most soldiers, he would rather have been fighting on the

Peninsula with the rest of his regiment than stuck at home training recruits. Especially now, when it seemed the war was close to ended and Boney almost beaten.

"Well, someone has already moved a couple of barrels," Paton said, obedient to his instructions. "When I first noticed them, I assumed his lordship had arranged for their delivery during his last visit, and thought no more of it until last night when I realized two were missing. Obviously, that could not have been his lordship since he is in London! That was when I opened the barrels to see what was in them."

"You could have knocked him down with a feather," Alice added, since she had escaped the schoolroom for luncheon.

Inevitably, the magistrate started asking the questions Serena already had and discovered that Paton had first noticed the cellar key to be missing the morning after his night off, which he'd spent at the Blackhaven Tavern.

"That place is a den of thieves and villains," Major Doverton exclaimed. "It should be shut down, Winslow!"

"But then where would your men drink?" Mr. Winslow said mildly. "To say nothing of the wild young gentlemen slumming it for an evening. I think instead, a subtle visit might be in order."

Major Doverton agreed reluctantly that this might be a more useful means of investigation. "I'd like to involve Colonel Fredericks, too," he added.

"Colonel Fredericks has retired," Serena objected, remembering the amiable old commander of the regiment whom she'd known for most of her life.

"Not entirely," Mr. Winslow said. "He still handles some important aspects of security, under the direct authority of the government."

"Really?" Serena was vastly intrigued, and eager to tell Tamar.

"Hmm," Winslow said thoughtfully. "I'd like you and your sisters to move out of the castle until this is over. Perhaps you could come and stay with us."

"Oh no, I thank you. We couldn't impose. Besides, if it's dangerous, doesn't it make more sense to remove the gunpowder?"

"The gunpowder is perfectly safe," Doverton said. "So long as you don't set fire to it! I think Mr. Winslow means that we shall set a trap for whoever is involved, and we don't want you here when they walk into it."

"But I would love to be here when they walk into it," Serena said, narrowing her eyes as she recalled the man who'd brandished the dagger at her and chased her through the woods. She pulled herself together. "I assure you we would not get in your way, and will stay inside the castle when you tell us. In fact, if we carry on as normal, surely it will be better for your plan? After all, we don't want them to know they are suspected."

Mr. Winslow tugged at his lower lip, clearly undecided.

"I would not take any chances with my sisters' safety, sir," she said quietly, and he looked from her to Alice and then to Doverton, who shrugged.

"Very well," Mr. Winslow said reluctantly. "But I don't want anybody outside after dark. If you go out for the evening, you must stay away until morning. My house is at your disposal, as I'm sure is the vicarage."

Doverton, who seemed to be regarding Serena now with more admiration than anything else, coughed and said, "I'll be sending men up here on watch, but they'll remain out of sight until they can trap the villains."

Serena nodded. "Will you follow them to see where they take the gunpowder?" she asked eagerly. "After all, they've already gone off with at least two barrels."

Again Mr. Winslow and the major exchanged glances. "That is a sensible idea," Doverton allowed. "If it can be done without putting your persons in danger."

THE GIRLS WERE released from their lessons just as Serena was donning her hat and pelisse to go for a stroll in the orchard. On one level, she ill-naturedly wished her sisters to Jericho. On another, she recognized that having them with her would be best. Whatever strange magnetism drew her and Tamar together physically, was just a little frightening—particularly when he'd made it clear he had no intention of offering marriage.

Besides, she couldn't send them away when they so clearly wanted to come.

"We could walk into Blackhaven," Helen suggested hopefully.

"We wouldn't be back before dark," Serena pointed out, "not unless we ran there and back without stopping. Let's just walk in the orchard."

"What's in the orchard?" Helen asked mutinously.

"Jem, apparently," Serena said as they approached. "Listen, he's arguing with someone."

"Oh Serena," Maria breathed. "Do you suppose it's *them?*"

Serena's heart lurched into her throat. "Surely not. It's still light." And Major Doverton's men were unlikely to arrive before dark. "You have to run," she said intensely, "as soon as I say so. Promise me."

Helen's hand slipped into hers. "As long as you come with us."

"Of course, I will. Carefully, then…" She opened the orchard door, and at once saw Jem half way up the central path.

Perched on a ladder against the largest apple tree, he was arguing with someone out of sight, but he didn't give the impression of fear or even true anger. Breathing more easily, she led the way in.

"Stay with me," she warned as Helen and Alice began to run ahead. The fact that they obeyed said more about their fears than their words had ever admitted. Perhaps she *should* send the girls and Miss Grey to the Winslows…

Jem caught sight of their approach and waved, another comforting sign. In fact, considering whom she had half-arranged to meet here, she was fairly sure before they even rounded the bend that it was Lord Tamar they would discover.

It was. He stood behind his easel, wearing his usual old coat, busily painting, although he spared a quick smile in their direction. The girls ran to him with every appearance of delight.

"I see you've met Jem," Serena said wryly.

"I've told him he's trespassing," Jem said at once. "But he says he has your permission to paint in the grounds. I thought he was lying."

"Well, I suppose I never said he couldn't," Serena said. "And since he seems to know everyone in Blackhaven, I doubt his lordship would object either. This is Lord Tamar."

"Are you sure?" Jem said dubiously. "He doesn't look much like a lord to me."

"He's an artist."

"So I see."

"Look, he's painted Jem!" Alice cried in delight. "With a cross face. Sir, will you paint us, too?"

"You can't afford me," Tamar said grandly.

Alice's face fell.

"I might as a present though, for your birthday," he added.

"Is Jem's a present, too, or can *he* afford you?" Helen asked.

"Of course, he can. Jem is a working man."

"I don't want my picture painted!" Jem exclaimed. "I only want to finish pruning this da—*wretched* tree before dark."

"Carry on, Jem," Serena said hastily. "Though I'm glad you're here because Lord Tamar is helping us with the barrel problem."

"How fares the barrel problem?" Tamar inquired.

Serena quickly told him what had transpired with Mr. Winslow and Major Doverton. While she talked, the girls admired his painting and then ran off, playing tag among the trees. It was good to see Maria forgetting the adult dignity she had begun to assume and play like a child once more. Serena had given up childhood too easily.

After a few moments observing them, she moved to take their place beside Tamar, watching him work.

His brush flew over the page, painting in the background with sure, swift strokes. While real life Jem returned to his work, it was the

Jem of the painting who kept drawing her gaze. Tamar had somehow caught both his irritation and his basic good nature. More than that, there was something noble in his poise, the way he was twisted round to look out of the picture, something idyllic about the whole scene.

"You're very good, aren't you?" she marveled. "Where did you study?"

He wrinkled his nose. "Tamar Abbey, largely. My father had left a huge collection of art materials there. I've no idea where they came from. I expect he won them from some poor devil in a card game. I just painted to amuse myself till a few people convinced me I was quite good. I got a few pointers from other artists who knew what they were doing, sold a couple of paintings to my neighbors and then had the idea of coming here to see if I could make any kind of living out of it."

"Can you?"

He shrugged. "I can feed myself, send a little home, but it's not enough to rebuild the estate, give my sister a dowry, or my brothers any kind of stable income."

"What do they do?" she asked curiously. "Your brothers?"

"Get into trouble, largely."

"Are you close?"

"God, no. We can't stand each other."

Serena blinked at this casual assertion. "And your sisters?"

"The twins aren't so bad. Christianne is still sweet enough to have caught a husband with prospects who doesn't give a fig for her poverty or her awful family. I like *your* family. Is your brother as good-natured?"

"Mostly." She wrinkled her nose. "Though he can be quite un-bending, which is how I come to be here in disgrace. I didn't do the right thing."

"Do you mean failing to marry the dull man who didn't make you happy? *Isn't* that the right thing?"

She blinked. "Put like that, I suppose it is. I wanted everyone to be proud of me, as they were of Frances. And Frances is happy. I assumed

I would be, too. I didn't think. I just obeyed, did what was expected. It didn't seem much of a burden at first. And then—" She broke off to tell the girls not to crash into Jem's ladder unless they wanted him to break a leg, and they ran further away from the apple tree.

"And then what?" Tamar prompted.

She sighed. "I suppose I'd grown discontented ever since Gillie married Wickenden. Gillie's an old friend, the daughter of one of the officers stationed here. She was not a great match for him by the world' standards. Conversely, he was considered a brilliant match for her. But none of that mattered to either of them, because they married for love. I saw it shining in her eyes and I knew beyond doubt that whatever duty, respect, or even liking I might feel for Sir Arthur, I would never have the kind of happiness Gillie had discovered."

He glanced up at her. "Is that what you were looking for with Dax?"

She shook her head impatiently. "I wasn't looking for anything with Dax. He just encouraged my natural *liveliness,* which had been so desperate to break out. I'm afraid I've always been too lively."

"No, you're not. It's part of your charm. Don't lose yourself to please anyone. It would be such a shame."

She brought her gaze from the picture, which she'd been staring at rather blindly for several moments, to his face. "*You* don't lose yourself, do you? You just do as you wish, whatever anyone's expectations of a peer."

"Well, to be fair, no one has any expectations of *this* peer, except that he will go to the devil faster than his father—having less money to prop him up."

She frowned. "But you're not going to the devil, are you? You're earning, looking after your family—to say nothing of me and mine!—and keeping your head above water. If you don't count the bailiff," she acknowledged.

His gaze dropped from hers to the painting. "Never discount the bailiff."

But she'd already glimpsed something in his face that caught at her breath, something that wasn't quite sadness or desperation or secrecy and yet, was made up of all three. She moved to see him better.

"There's something you're not telling me," she said.

"Many, many things. My life is not a book written for well-bred young ladies."

"No, there's more," she said with certainty. "You give no details about your family, you turn the subject when I speak of them—"

"So would you if you had my family." Selecting a different paint brush, he began to add detail to the fallen leaves in his picture.

"And the bailiff cannot touch you," she blurted. "You're a peer of the realm. Why do you keep up such a fiction?"

"To make myself seem interesting. Actually, I'm not really Tamar at all. I just pretend so I'll be invited to parties."

"Are you?"

"Sometimes. Blackhaven seems to like me."

She scowled at him. "I meant, as you very well know, are you really the Marquis of Tamar?"

"If I wasn't, I'd sweep you off your feet and marry you out of hand." At last, his gaze came back to her, warm and deliberately distracting. She knew that, and yet it didn't stop the butterflies soaring in her stomach or the memory of his passionate kisses.

"Why?" she managed. "Why is it worse to be a marquis? To be *this* marquis? What have you done?"

If there was any thought behind her questions, it was to taunt him, goad him into telling her the truth. She wasn't prepared for the rush of emotion, of absolute fury and misery that spilled from his eyes, before his thick, black lashes swept down, hiding them.

He threw down his brush, began packing his palette and brushes and rags into his satchel. "The light is fading. Jem has finished his work, and you must take your sisters back to the house."

"You're dismissing me!" she said, in outraged frustration.

He laughed, swinging the satchel over his shoulder. "Oh, my dear, it's the best I can possibly do for you."

"Lord Tamar, play tag with us!" Helen panted, running up to

them, Alice and Maria at her heels.

"Next time," he said, covering the painting. "I have to go, and so do you."

"But you will paint us?" Alice pursued.

"Of course, I will. One day." Easel and picture under his arm, he cast them a comical bow. "Farewell, young ladies. Lady Serena, your servant." At last, a quick, faint smile lit his eyes. "I am that, at least." And then he was striding off toward the upper door, calling to Jem as he went.

Serena felt as if she'd been pushed over and trampled. Worse, she had the awful feeling that she'd driven him away, that she'd never see him again.

Chapter Eight

S INCE THE NEXT day was Saturday, when the girls did not have
formal lessons, Serena agreed they should walk into Blackhaven
and enjoy an ice at the parlor which had sprung up at the bottom end
of the high street.

"Would you like to come with us, Miss Grey?" she asked the governess. "Or would you rather enjoy the time alone?"

The governess appeared to hesitate.

"Either is fine," Serena assured her. "Your company is always welcome, but you are more than entitled to a day away from us."

She'd never said such a thing to a governess before, let alone
meant it. But she genuinely liked Miss Grey and so did the girls. They
were lucky to have her.

"To be honest, what I would really like is a long walk in the country," Miss Grey confessed. "It's such a beautiful autumn day."

"By all means," Serena said. "I'll have Cook pack you up some
luncheon if you wish. Only *please* don't get lost! And be sure to return
before dark as we've all been warned."

Last night had been quiet, with no sounds of intrusion or pursuit,
and when Paton had checked the cellar that morning, there was no
change in the number of foreign barrels stored there. Which was a bit
of an anti-climax, although the danger was hardly over.

"Of course," Miss Grey assured her.

Serena smiled and walked away, but as if plucking up her courage,
the governess detained her. "Lady Serena?"

"Yes?" She turned back, expectantly in time to see Miss Grey taking a hesitant step toward her.

"My lady, I know it is not my place to speak, and I really do trust your judgment, only—"

Serena frowned. "Only what?"

"It's about Lord Tamar," Miss Grey said in a rush. She came closer, meeting Serena's surprised gaze. "Have you considered that *he* might be part of this gunpowder plot of ours?"

Serena blinked. "No," she said baldly.

"Well, as a I say, I trust your judgment. It's just that…it came to me last night when I was trying to go back to sleep. You were chased by a man with a knife and ran into Lord Tamar. You waited in the cellar for the smugglers to appear—and Lord Tamar did."

Something nasty clawed at Serena's stomach. Her instinct was simply to dismiss Miss Grey's suspicions out of hand, for she knew Tamar had nothing to do with those incidents, except in so far as he'd helped her. And yet Miss Grey's words were perfectly true. And Miss Grey was both clever and perceptive.

"No," Serena said at last. "If he'd been involved, why would he have shown me the barrels contained gunpowder? Why would he have bothered to be kind to me if he'd just tried to kill me?"

"I don't know," Miss Grey said miserably. "I know he is a likeable man, and I can see no motive for his kindness if he is our villain. Only…only, he is a poor man, and might well be induced to act against his conscience for money. People do."

Serena thought, frowning. To some extent, the governess's suspicions made sense. Just not when she considered the man she was coming to know.

"No," she said firmly. "You're wrong. But I appreciate your looking out for us."

DESPITE AN INITIAL tendency of Alice and Helen to quarrel during their walk, Serena had coaxed everyone into good humor well before they reached the town.

"We could call on Lord Tamar," Helen suggested.

Serena, who, despite Miss Grey's warnings, had every desire to see both the artist and his studio, murmured that that would not be quite proper. She had a horror of imposing, of reading too much into the bold flirtation of an unconventional man. She did not want to see annoyance in his eyes if she disturbed him in his lair. And after their last encounter, she was very much afraid she would.

"But after we've had an ice, we should probably call at the vicarage," she said brightly.

The vicarage was clearly considered to be a poor substitute for the artist's studio, but since ices were the first order of the day, no one complained. Yet.

Their little group caused quite a stir in Blackhaven. Most of the long-time residents knew who they were and greeted them in friendly spirit, usually bowing. The visitors, who seemed to grow in number every time Serena came home, regarded them with curiosity and whispers, although one or two whom Serena recognized from London, did come and speak a few courteous words.

Serena joined her sisters in a dish of delicious ices. "This is as good as anything at Gunthers, don't you think?" she enthused.

The girls agreed readily, comparing favorite flavors with the palates of connoisseurs. They were so engaged when a gentleman came in and bowed to them.

"Why, Monsieur de Valère," Serena greeted him in surprise. "I did not imagine you to be much of an ice man."

"I'm not," he confessed. "I merely saw you through the window and came in to pay my respects."

"How civil of you. Allow me to present my sisters, Lady Maria, Alice, and Helen. Girls, M. le Comte de Valère, who is a friend of the Winslows."

"And of yours, I trust," Valère protested.

The comte only stayed to exchange a few words and then politely took his leave.

"Is he another admirer of yours?" Maria asked.

"Why, no, though he may be of Catherine Winslow." She frowned. "What do you mean, *another* admirer?"

"As well as Lord Tamar. And it seems to me the comte admires you, too."

"You're being silly," Serena said, for some reason uncomfortable about both gentlemen.

"No, she isn't." Alice argued. "But I like Lord Tamar better."

"Because he's English?" Serena teased.

"No, because—"

"In any case, you're talking nonsense," Serena interrupted. "Come, let's look in the shops, then see if Mrs. Grant is at home. We can walk home by way of the harbor and the beach, if the tide is far enough out."

After spending some time in the book shop and buying some new ribbon for Maria's hair, they walked round to the vicarage. Kate appeared delighted to see them, and Mr. Grant even emerged from his study—where he claimed to have been writing tomorrow's sermon—to join them for tea and cake.

"So what is next?" he asked. "More wicked dissipation in Blackhaven? Or the long walk home?"

"We thought we'd walk along the beach and up the cliff paths," Serena said.

"Though we'd quite like to call on Lord Tamar first," Helen said defiantly. "We'd like to see his paintings, but Serena says it wouldn't be proper to call."

"It probably would, if we came with you," Kate said unexpectedly, and in spite of her best intentions, Serena's heart began to beat with hope.

"Or just you," Mr. Grant said to his wife, "for I have to call in on Lampton. But you could take Tamar a message from me…"

"How do they know Tamar?" Kate asked with deceptive casualness as they walked together round to the harbor. "Did he call on you at the castle?"

"Not exactly," Serena said cautiously. "It seems he's in the habit of trespassing there to paint."

"And we're having an adventure with him," Helen said happily. Maria glared at her. "What?"

"Indeed?" Kate said pleasantly. "What kind of adventure?"

"One involving gunpowder," Serena said, giving in to the inevitable. The whole story then came out in hushed tones.

"Goodness," Kate said faintly. "For such a small town, there is rarely a dull moment in Blackhaven."

Arriving at the harbor, they turned left along the shore road where a row of fishermen's cottages stood. A man in an ill-made coat sat on the steps of one, one leg stretched out in front of him as he contemplated the sea. Neither gentleman nor fisherman, by his dress, he looked quite out of place in this neighborhood.

"Goodness," Kate said in startled tones. "He *does* have a bailiff."

"*This* is Lord Tamar's studio?" Serena wasn't quite sure what she'd expected.

"It is." Without any more warning, Kate stopped at the front step, regarding the bailiff, who looked back with insolent curiosity. She had suddenly assumed a manner much more reminiscent of the superior, intimidating Kate Serena remembered.

"My good man," she drawled. "You must be aware you have no business with a peer of the realm. Be off with you before I call the watch."

The bailiff jumped to his feet, looking as if he wished to say something rude or defiant. And then he simply effaced himself.

"Good," Kate said with satisfaction and sailed up to the front door. She rapped it with the handle of her umbrella. Receiving no response, she called, "Tamar, I know you're in there. I have a message from the vicar!"

Even from the step, Serena heard Tamar's muffled snort of laughter. An instant later, the key turned in the lock and the door was thrown open to reveal Lord Tamar in his shirt sleeves, with his hair even more tousled than usual. He wore no necktie and his shirt front hung half-open to reveal the strong column of his throat and a tantalizing glimpse of manly chest and shoulder.

Serena felt a blush begin somewhere near her toes and rise upward with alarming speed, but it seemed Tamar was even more stunned by the deputation at his door.

"Good God," he uttered.

"Alas, not even the vicar," Kate said flippantly. "The young ladies would very much like to see your paintings. Lady Serena and I are here to chaperone them."

Tamar's gaze skimmed past Serena, as if he couldn't bear to look at her, and her heart sank. She should never have pushed him yesterday. Whatever his secrets, he didn't want them prodded, certainly not by her. She wished she hadn't come.

Tamar, peering beyond the step, said, "What have you done with my bailiff?"

"Kate sent him about his business," Serena said lightly.

"Clearly, I should have sent for you weeks ago."

"You're more than capable of getting rid of him yourself, if you wish to," Kate retorted. "Particularly since he can't legally arrest you."

"Ah, but he is useful to me," Tamar said, apparently not in the least put-out. "He fends off other vermin."

"Oh goodness," Helen said, looking around in awe.

"You mean the mess or the pictures?" he asked carelessly. "You have my permission to kick aside anything that is not a painting. It's what I do. I can't offer you refreshment ladies, unless your tastes run to brandy?"

"No, I thank you," Kate said. "You should have someone to clean for you."

"Are you offering?" Tamar asked outrageously.

"What other vermin?" Serena blurted.

Tamar's unreadable gaze focused on her. One eyebrow lifted quizzically.

"What other vermin does your supposed bailiff fend off?" she asked more clearly.

She expected an evasion at best, but again he surprised her. "Ah, there's another mystery. Some of my paintings have vanished and it strikes me it might be *his* fault that more haven't been taken."

Serena frowned. "Because no one can get past him without being seen? Perhaps he's in league with the thief."

"I wouldn't put it past the thief," he allowed, "but perhaps the bailiff has standards. Did anything happen last night at the castle?"

"No, it was quite dull," Serena replied. "Have you lost many paintings?"

"A few landscapes and the portrait of Dax and his lady." He moved away from her, throwing a large, paint-covered cloth over the canvas currently on the easel by the window, the one Kate was walking toward. The vicar's wife stuck her tongue out at him.

"What is he doing with them?" Serena asked, gazing at a rather beautiful picture of Brathwaite Castle at sunset.

"Selling them. Certainly, he sold one at the local gallery, pretending to be acting for me." Tamar grimaced. "Negotiated a better price, too, damn him. I expect that's what is paying to send the other paintings elsewhere by some means or another." In one movement, he swept a newspaper, two books, and a small pile of indistinguishable clothing off the sofa, then kicked it all forcefully to one side. "Please, sit down," he invited.

"That's outrageous," Kate observed, sitting gracefully. "Set the watch on him. Mr. Winslow would be happy to organize that for you."

"No point, really, I know who it is. I just don't know what he's done with them. I need him to lead me to Daxton's portrait at the very least. It's meant to be a wedding gift. What *is* Grant's message, by the way?"

"*Not in Carlisle,*" Kate quoted wryly. "Does that refer to your paintings? My husband does play his cards very close to his chest at times."

"I asked him to," Tamar apologized.

"Maybe York then," Kate suggested. "Or London. Though who but Daxton's family would want a portrait of Dax? I'm fairly sure

Willa's family wouldn't!"

"He won't know it's anyone as famous—or infamous—as Dax. He probably just thinks it's a pretty picture he can sell."

Serena, after watching her sisters rummage through the paintings piled along the walls with a modicum of care, sat down beside Kate. "Is it?"

His gaze landed on her face. So did Kate's.

She flushed. "I mean, here, you are known and your paintings have come to be valued. And while I know there is some coming and going between Blackhaven and London, I am wondering if your thief will find the pictures as easy to sell there. You say you know who the thief is. Does he have knowledge of the London art world? Acquaintances there?"

"I would doubt it," Tamar said thoughtfully, his gaze remaining on her face. "Although one can never tell."

She drew in her breath. "Perhaps you should go to London," she said in a rush.

His lips twisted. "Perhaps I should. Only then, who would prevent him plundering my studio at his leisure? Even my bailiff would follow me."

"You mean the thief is still here in Blackhaven?" Kate asked in surprise.

"He arrived on the stagecoach and he hasn't left again. Nor has he hired a horse, so yes, I think he's still here."

"You need to have him arrested," Serena said with decision. "Then, even if he won't tell what he's done with the paintings, at least he won't take any more."

"It would give me a certain amount of satisfaction," Tamar admitted. "But I find I'm loathe to drag his name through the mud."

"Why?"

He laughed. "Because it's the same as mine. The thief is my brother."

Serena stared at him in horror. Beside her, she was sure Kate's face bore much the same expression. From nowhere, she remembered the man she'd seen in the gallery who at first glance had looked so much like Tamar. Could that have been his brother? The thief? Surely no one would steal from his own brother! Certainly not one as good-natured as Tamar. Or was he too good-natured? Did this betrayal *hurt* him?

"How do you know?" Serena demanded. "How do you know it was your brother? Do you have proof?"

"He gave his name to Davidson at the gallery. Davidson described him. And the tavern staff know him by the same name."

"It could be a trick to deceive you into leaving him alone," Kate said hopefully. "Perhaps he gave a false name."

"Oh, he did. He gave the name of my youngest brother, to send me on a false trail after Sylvester."

Serena frowned in bewilderment. "How do you know it *isn't* Sylvester?"

He threw up one impatient hand. "Because Sylvester isn't that devious. He'd clear the paintings out in one swoop and probably leave me a note. Julian prefers to entertain himself."

"But he must know there's a risk of your discovering him," Serena objected. "Especially if he's still staying at the tavern."

"Well, there's the thing. He isn't. I went to his room and there's no sign of him. His bed hadn't been slept in. There are no clothes there and certainly no paintings.

"Then he must be at the hotel." Kate said. "There's nowhere else *to* stay in Blackhaven."

"He isn't. I doubt he can afford the hotel," Tamar said impatiently. "Not with the sale of one painting." He blinked suddenly, then began to laugh. He threw himself on to the stool near the covered easel "What am I saying? He *is* still here, and I think I know why. Don't worry. If I'm right, I'll get all the paintings back." His eyes refocused on Serena, then shifted to Kate. "Sorry. Now you know more than you ever wanted to about my family. Feel free to cut me at any time."

"I think I'll just have a look at your paintings, first," Serena said, jumping to her feet. For some reason, his squalid little story had only increased her curiosity in his work. While she wandered around, gazing at the paintings hanging on the cluttered walls, crouching down to examine those propped up on the floor, the girls bombarded him with questions. Who were the people in the portraits or depicted in landscapes? Which ship was that in the harbor, whose was the house? Tamar answered them all with a mixture of honesty and wild, stories that had them in stitches.

"Why, this is Haven House," Maria said once. "Is it really so over-grown, now? Is there not a new tenant there?"

"Yes, but he seems to like it this way," Tamar said. "It can't be very comfortable, of course, but I thought it made an interesting painting." He lowered his voice, contorting his body. "A haunted house."

The girls giggled.

For Serena, the more she looked at his work, the more impressed she became by his talent. It was far more than technical competence, which in itself would have been impressive enough considering his lack of formal training. He had the knack of capturing an atmosphere, complicated expressions, the beauty in everyday objects as well as in people the world regarded as nobodies, even ugly nobodies.

There was one painting hanging up, of an old woman collecting wood in the forest at the edge of a lake. The loveliness of the lush, local countryside was staggering. In such a piece, Serena would have expected the poor old woman to be part of the background, but she wasn't. She was the focus of his painting, bent and wrinkled and ragged. And yet, there was charm in her eyes, in the exquisite structure of her bones, in the very character of her face, old in experience, both tragic and happy. He'd seen beneath the ugliness of age to the beauty of her life, her person, and more than that, he'd shown it to whoever looked.

It made her want to cry, that picture. Tamar was more, far more, than the amiable, careless young man he appeared. His perception, his understanding, staggered her, set her wondering afresh what experi-ence had forged it.

And somewhere, too, it saddened her. No wonder he rejected her tentative overtures. What was there in her silly, shallow life of privilege, parties, and husband-hunting to capture the genuine interest of such a man? She was well aware she could inspire attention, even lust, although she was not meant to know about such things. She'd had a taste of Tamar's. But that was not enough to keep him.

The pain turned her away from the painting, but she hadn't taken a step before her eyes strayed back to it.

"My lord, what would you charge for this?" she blurted.

"Take it," he said at once. Leaving the girls clustered with Kate over some local scenes, he strolled across to see, presumably, which picture she meant.

"You'll never make any money if you give away all your master-pieces," she said severely.

He stood behind her, a little to one side, and every nerve tingled with awareness. His warmth, his clean yet earthy scent filled her.

"You like that one?" he said in surprise.

"It makes me sad and happy at once. Who is she?"

"Her name is Martha. I met her on my way up here, not so far from Blackhaven. Formidable woman." His breath stirred the hairs on her neck.

She swallowed. "Will you sell it to me?"

"Of course." He reached over her head to take the picture down.

She wanted to whisk herself under his arm to get away. She longed to stay this way forever, to keep this intimacy, this promise that there could be more between them. His chest brushed against her shoulder, her hair. There seemed to be some difficulty with the hanging wire being caught around the nail in the wall, which caused a delay. Imagining this would be absorbing all his attention, she risked a surreptitious glance at his face... and met his steady gaze.

Her heart seemed to dive. She couldn't breathe. The moment stretched. Because she couldn't help it, she dropped her gaze to his slightly parted lips, became fascinated with every tiny crease in their texture. It would take so little to reach up and touch them with her own, to step back fully against him and feel his arms close around her.

He moved, freeing the picture from its nail at last, but though he straightened behind her once more, he didn't step back, merely held the picture out to her.

Swallowing, she took it. "Thank you." It came out as a whisper, appalling her. Pride decreed she should hide his effect upon her.

His lips quirked, but he said nothing. He stepped back at last, giving space to Helen and Kate who had come to see what she'd chosen. Mutely, she held out the painting, to let them see for themselves. She couldn't trust herself to speak, for the tiny incident had shaken her to her core.

THEY LEFT WITH two paintings, having also taken the one of Braithwaite Castle at sunset as a gift for Gervaise. Although the girls had made a wish list as long as their own arms, they didn't have the funds to buy, and Serena refused to countenance any presents from the marquis.

To her surprise, as they took their leave, Tamar slung on his coat to accompany them and carry the roughly wrapped paintings—which was kind, for although the castle one was fairly small and light, the old lady was large and framed.

They parted from Kate at the harbor, though only after the vicar's wife had promised the children to think about playing chaperone at the castle so that Tamar could paint their portraits.

"You don't need to do such a thing," Serena assured him as they walked down the steps to the beach. "I'm not even sure Braithwaite will fork out for it."

"Oh well, it will be more fun than my mill owner, in any case. I would like to paint them."

"I think you want to paint everyone and everything."

"Sometimes, I do," he admitted. "Other times, nothing inspires me. It's already there, so why paint it? Why make it less than it already is?"

"I don't think you ever do that."

He glanced at her. "You're being kind."

"No."

After the odd moment in his studio and the manner of their previous parting, she thought there might be some awkwardness between them. But his mood seemed to change like quicksilver—from the brooding cynic he'd portrayed when they first arrived at the studio, to the fun, surrogate brother he'd been to the girls, to the intense man who'd stared at her like a lover. And now this carefree friend who told them to take off their shoes and run in the sand, for no one would see them.

When he sat down on the beach, the pictures balanced on his thighs while he kicked off his boots and stockings, Serena and the girls sat behind him to remove their own. With delicacy, he stood and walked on, waiting until the girls ran up to him. Then, he tapped Helen on the shoulder.

"Tag!" he said, and darted away at high speed, the pictures still under his arm along with his boots. All the girls ran after him, including Serena, and there ensued a fast and spirited game of tag that took them breathless and laughing, all the way round to Braithwaite Cove.

"The tide's coming in," Maria observed. "You won't be able to go back along the beach. He can have tea with us at the castle, can't he, Serena? Since he'll have to come up with us anyway to get to the road."

"Does your cook make chocolate cake every day?" he asked with every appearance of hope.

"No, sometimes she makes a lemon cake which is almost as good," Helen said. "And a cherry cake…"

"Well, you must have made him so hungry by now that he won't survive without tea," Serena said lightly. He'd been in the kitchen the other night, after all. He seemed to have a knack of eroding society's boundaries. But surely, if Miss Grey was home, there was no real harm.

Chapter Nine

TAMAR KNEW HE shouldn't go in. Quite aside from whatever trouble she'd get into with her brother and the countess for receiving visitors of his reputation, he knew that he was getting in far too deep. Every moment spent in her company would make the inevitable parting harder, possibly for them both. He could tell himself it was making them familiar and therefore boring to each other, extinguishing this fascination by a hearty dose of the mundane and civilized. But in his heart, he knew he was beguiled by the innocent fun of the family, perhaps because it was something like his own might have been, if only things had been different.

And he was more than beguiled by Serena. He wanted her, of course. He always had. Her beauty, her wit, and sheer vitality had charmed him from the outset. But he'd never imagined she'd weep for old Martha of the Lakes, as he called the woman of the painting Serena had bought. *She makes me sad and happy at once.* He'd seen the tears standing in her eyes. She felt what he had. His painting had made her feel it, and he treasured that.

You're attributing affinity where there is none, he told himself severely. *Because you want it to be there.*

It didn't matter. He found himself walking into the castle through the front door, following the young ladies past the Friday-faced butler.

"Thank you, Paton," Serena said. "We'll all have tea in the small drawing room. Is Miss Grey back yet?"

"Just ten minutes ago, my lady."

"Ask her to join us, if you please." Tossing her pelisse over the butler's waiting arm with a smile that must have endeared her to all her servants, she led the way up the grand staircase to a long gallery, lined with portraits of past earls. At least, he assumed that's who they were, for he followed her into the drawing room before he'd glimpsed more than a few stern faces.

A fire had been lit in the grate. To his surprise, Serena knelt on the rug before it and raised her arms to receive the pictures. It was such a natural gesture, he could imagine her holding her arms up like this to ask for his embrace.

Mentally squashing the vision, he laid the pictures before her on the rug instead and unwrapped them.

The younger ladies were debating where they should be hung when the governess walked into the room. Called upon, she duly admired the paintings, though she seemed distracted by more than Tamar's somewhat unconventional presence at tea.

Since the maids almost immediately brought in tea, newly baked bread and butter, scones and a cake that made the girls' eyes sparkle, no one questioned Miss Grey until the servants had retired. Serena, from a more traditional position in an arm chair, poured the tea for Alice to take to everyone, while Helen and Maria offered plates of bread and scones.

From long habit in never being sure where his next meal would come from, Tamar took two slices of bread and a scone.

"Are you quite well, Miss Grey?" Serena asked. "Did you not have a pleasant walk?"

"Yes, of course I am," Miss Grey replied in surprise, "and my walk was most pleasant indeed. For most of the day, I did not see a soul, except a few farmers in the distance. Only then I did encounter a strange man and have been debating with myself ever since whether or not I should tell you."

"Why?" Serena asked blankly.

"Because of our current...problems," Miss Grey said with delicacy. "With gunpowder and so on. And I'm very aware Mr. Winslow said to be wary of strangers."

"Did he threaten you?" Maria demanded.

"No, no, not in the slightest. He was merely…grumpy. But he clearly didn't want anyone on that land, whether it was his own or his employer's. He sent me the other way. And I wondered if perhaps our villains were hiding up there. Only he didn't appear terribly villainous."

"Where was this?" Serena demanded.

From Miss Grey's slightly erratic description of her path, Tamar surmised she'd been near Haven Hall. "What did he look like?" he asked.

"Tall, with hair as black as yours, sir. And a scar running all the way down his right cheek."

"Oh, he sounds most villainous," Alice enthused.

"He sounds most like the tenant of Haven Hall," Tamar said wryly. "I met him walking up there, too."

"Then you don't think he has anything to do with our gunpowder?" Serena asked, as though disappointed.

Tamar scratched his head. "I would doubt it, though I suppose it isn't impossible. No one seems to know where he's come from and he has no obvious connection to the area. He certainly doesn't mingle with the community."

"Perhaps we should call on him," Serena mused.

"I will," Tamar said hastily. "He'd think it dashed odd if a parcel of young ladies and their governess just turned up on his doorstep!" Having finished his scone, he reached for another.

"Perhaps he means to blow up Haven Hall," Helen said hopefully.

"Why would he do that?" Alice scoffed.

"I don't know. Why would anyone have gunpowder here? Unless they were soldiers, and we know it doesn't belong to the 44th."

Tamar had his own theory about that, though he chose to keep it to himself. He knew he'd feel much easier when the owners of the powder were safely locked up.

From somewhere in his childhood, he dredged up enough idea of etiquette not to linger too long at the castle, tempting as it was. After a second cup of tea and a slice of the lightest, tastiest fruit cake he'd ever eaten, he rose and civilly took his leave.

"You will come back tomorrow to paint us?" Helen said anxiously.

"If Mrs. Grant can spare the time," he promised. "I will."

"What about *your* time," Serena asked as she accompanied him downstairs. In spite of everything, he was glad she did. "Don't you want to pursue your missing paintings?"

"I think I know what Julian's waiting for," he said. "I'll check in Blackhaven, but I think I have a few days' grace."

She nodded. She hadn't rung for a servant and there were none in sight as they walked across the hall. It didn't matter, he still had his coat and he rarely wore his one, battered hat.

She smiled and offered him her hand. "Thank you for the paintings."

"Thank you for buying them." He took her hand and bowed over it.

"They're worth more," she said.

The words didn't really matter. Though he should have released it long since, he still held her hand. It was another of those moments, like the one in the studio, when he'd reached above her head for the picture, when he could have pulled her back against him and ravished her. Her bare, elegant neck had tempted him to do just that, if only they had been alone. He'd burned for her, then. He still did, God help him.

He needed to end this.

Why then, was he raising her hand to his lips, turning it so that he could kiss the inside of her wrist? He made it a lingering kiss that drank in the hammering of her pulse under his mouth.

She wanted him.

Her breasts rose and fell with such alluring rapidity that he barely kept from crushing her in his arms, from thrusting his hand over her heart to feel its thunder, to cup a sweet, soft breast...

He swallowed. If he didn't say it now, he never would. "Goodbye, Serena."

And then, it seemed, he could drop her hand, though afterward, he'd no recollection of how he'd got out of the house. He was just grateful for the cold on his face and for the long coat and the gathering darkness to hide his raging arousal.

Avoiding the busiest parts of town, he strode along side streets toward the harbor, wondering if he should blow his last few pennies on ale at the tavern.

"My lord, have I offended you somehow?" The teasing voice interrupted his determinedly narrow thoughts. Since the voice was familiar, he paused, refocusing on the young woman who'd addressed him.

"Linnet," he said, initially more pleased by his ability to recall her name than by her actual presence. Which was hardly kind of him considering the intimacy they'd shared on more than one occasion. She was an actress and dancer at the theatre.

She laughed. "You were miles away. A penny for your thoughts!"

"Alas, you'd waste your money, for they're worthless. Merely the great debate of the evening—tavern or not."

"You could give up on the tavern and take me for supper at the hotel instead," she suggested boldly.

He gave a lopsided smile. "Nothing would give me greater pleasure. However, sadly, my pockets are to let." He frowned. "Talking of the hotel, though... you wouldn't happen to know when the next gaming club night is happening there?"

"I believe it's tomorrow night. But you can't play there without a *considerable* amount of money! The stakes are high."

"Oh, I know. But there's free wine and supper, is there not?"

She took his arm in a familiar manner. "There, you are always hungry! Come, step round to my rooms and I'll cook you some supper tonight."

Tamar was touched. She seemed to genuinely like him, since the world knew he hadn't two pennies to rub together. And it wasn't pity that stood out in her pretty, eager eyes. She was offering more than supper, and he already knew she was a pleasing and adventurous lover.

Temptation screamed through his body. It had been on fire all afternoon, ever since Serena Conway had walked into his studio, and here before him was a pretty, willing woman in whom he could happily sate himself.

Shame forced its way into his heart. He didn't want Linnet. She deserved more, far more for her kindness and affection than a man who used her.

Besides, some strange, unknown part of him was insisting he be true to Serena. Why, he had no idea, since there were certainly no promises between them, nor likely to be. He was obsessed, God help him.

And yet, his body screamed at him to accept the offered oblivion of lust.

"I can't," he said ruefully. "But you've no idea how grateful I am for the kindness."

The light in her eyes died away to disappointment.

"Linnet," he said low. "I have nothing to offer any woman, but friendship."

Her smile was brave. "I'll take it."

He considered. "Then… if you'd care to help me out, you could accompany me to the club tomorrow evening?"

She frowned. "I thought you'd nothing to play with?"

"Oh, I'm not going to play. And given my notorious poverty, I need a reason to be there."

"Me?" she said cynically, her frown deepening. "I've no idea why I like you, Tamar, unless it's your brutal honesty. I'll come."

He smiled, tipped his imaginary hat to her, and bowed.

The man he thought of so disparagingly as the bum-bailiff, sat once more on his doorstep. But Tamar was in no mood to avoid him. He'd had enough of Rivers. One way or another, his siblings could all look after themselves. Even Anna. Especially Anna.

But more than either of those, he began to see desperation in the bailiff's continued presence here in the dark, even after Kate Grant had sent him away with a flea in his ear. The balance of power between them had shifted subtly.

"Got something for me?" Rivers inquired, without getting up as Tamar approached the step.

"No. Nor will I have. Go away."

"You *want* to face the consequences of not paying your debt?"

"I owe you no debt." Tamar walked up the side of the steps as if he wasn't there. "Go away."

"Lot of good people here will be shocked," Rivers said.

Tamar laughed and inserted his key in the lock. "Go away, Rivers. Those good people really will call the Watch on you."

IT WAS DURING the evening that another truth began to dawn on him.

By candlelight, he was gazing at the portraits of Serena, lost in the work he ached to be doing on them if only he had enough light. Wrapped in the warmth she always brought him, his thoughts all centered on her until they began to include her worries. Gunpowder.

It was a bizarre thing to smuggle into the country at Blackhaven, but if one wasn't buying it from legal sources, there had to be a reason. An illegal reason. Robbery, perhaps, although gunpowder was a somewhat drastic—and loud—means of entry. Sabotage? There was no shortage of discontent in the country, but Blackhaven and its environs were hardly a seat of political power. Or industrial wealth. It was some considerable distance to the major mill towns of Manchester and the rest, and no one seemed to be in a great hurry to move the stuff.

Blackhaven, of course, was not as well guarded as the southern coasts. And the smugglers weren't only English. He'd heard about the spy discovered at the barracks that spring, who'd been working to escape to France via a French smuggling vessel.

But what else could the French want from here? For what purpose could they possibly want several barrels of hidden gunpowder?

The prison.

The idea hit him in a flash, with such force that he lowered his brush. French prisoners-of-war were kept in a fort ten miles or so outside Blackhaven. The gunpowder could well be intended to break in to the fort and free the prisoners. If that were true, then it better explained the attack on Serena. They were desperate, had no interest in her exalted identity, were possibly even French soldiers.

Tamar rocked back on his stool and threw down his brush. Jumping up, he seized his coat and rushed outside, barely remembering to lock the door behind him. About to leap down the front steps, he nearly tripped over a solid figure sitting there.

"God damn you," he cursed. "*Will* you go away?"

"Not without my money," Rivers said stubbornly.

"Do I look like a man with any money? Do yourself a favor—go and work for it. At least you'll have control of that, and trust me, Rivers, you have none over me."

With that, he hurried up the road, aiming for the barracks and Major Doverton.

TAMAR, HAVING TRIPPED over the body, risked uncovering one side of the lantern to see who it was.

A uniformed soldier fluttered his eyelids in the sudden brightness and groaned.

"He's not dead," Tamar said in relief. "But there's blood coming from his head."

"Cobbler, sit up and talk to me," Major Doverton snapped without notable sympathy. "Or there will be more blood! What happened to you?"

Tamar had seized upon the major just as he was about to leave to check on his castle patrol. Accompanying him, Tamar had told him his theory about the French and the prison, and Doverton certainly hadn't dismissed it. In fact, he'd appeared to have been mulling it over when they encountered the body at the foot of the hill.

Cobbler sat up groggily, clutching his head, and groaned again. "Christ, my head." Mouth open, he blinked from Doverton to Tamar and then took in his surroundings as illuminated by the lantern. His frown deepened. "Damn it, what am I doing here? I was at the top of the hill...Someone hit me!"

"Never," Doverton said sarcastically. "Cobbler, who hit you? And how?"

Cobbler dropped his gaze. "Sneaked up on me," he muttered. "Never heard a thing, then I got this feeling—you know, when all the hairs stand up on the back of your neck? I looked over my shoulder, there was this shadow and then—*whack!*" Gingerly, he felt the back of his head and his scowl deepened. "Bastard kicked me down the hill. I remember falling and couldn't stop myself."

"Where did he go?" Doverton demanded. "How many of them were there?"

"I don't know!" Cobbler exclaimed.

"Well, we know where they went," Tamar said grimly, already striding up the hill. He just hoped he wasn't too late, that the castle doors remained locked and its occupants safe.

Serena, her head full of Lord Tamar, couldn't sleep.

She'd hung his painting of the old woman on the wall to her left, beside the window, and for a while she lay with her bed curtains open on that side, gazing at the painting in the candlelight. She drank in all the sadness and joy it inspired in her. Like Tamar himself. She'd never felt so alive as she did in his company, so churned up and wonderful and frightened, so glad and yet so in need. He was *life* to her.

Oh goodness, she thought, suddenly breathless. *Is that it? Is that why I feel as I do? Do I love* him?

The huge, terrifying thought filled her, overwhelmed her, until she realized that the very idea made her happy. She barely knew him, and she was honest enough to acknowledge that tomorrow or the next day, the feeling might not be there. But even this glimpse, this possibility, gave her something to aim for in life.

Frances had been lucky in her husband. Had Serena married Sir Arthur Maynard, she wouldn't have been. They would have made each other miserable, and Serena knew as well as she knew anything, that unhappiness would have made her behave badly. It had already begun the night she'd danced with Lord Daxton.

Marriage. Marriage to Tamar would be *fun*. They understood each other, shared their sense of the ridiculous. And he set her senses alight. Her body, her whole being sang when she was near him. Money didn't matter. She would find a way, if only he cared for her in the same way.

But she was rushing again. She needed to be calm and wait and see if the feeling stayed, if it grew or if it faded and died. Even if it did die, even if they could never be together for whatever reason, she couldn't regret feeling as she did. She couldn't regret loving him whether for this night, this week, or forever.

Smiling with sheer happiness, she blew out the candle and lay down to sleep. She hoped she would dream of him.

But her heart and mind were too full to let her settle. She tossed and turned and waited restlessly for sleep to take her. And so, she was awake to hear the whispering in the courtyard. For a moment, she thought she'd misheard some rustling, but no, it came again, followed by a very faint scrape. Like a key in a lock.

Hastily, she jumped out of bed, dragging a blanket with her to throw around her shoulders. Finding the curtain by feel, she swished it aside and sat in the window seat, pressing her nose to the glass and peering downward.

"*Vite!*" came a hoarsely whispered instruction. "*Allez!*"

A couple of shadowy figures moved at the edge of her vision, and then there was silence.

French. They were speaking in French!

The combination of gunpowder and her country's enemies was truly frightening. She actually stood up, meaning to rush down and lock them in the cellar if she could, though fortunately, she remembered the plan. The authorities had to find the rest of the gunpowder in case there were others free to use it.

She sank back onto the window seat, scanning the ground above the yard for any signs of the soldiers Major Doverton had promised. He'd said they would be hidden, and certainly she couldn't make anybody out.

The idea of the enemy in the cellar below, chilled her blood.

But she did not have long to wait. Before long, a man emerged from the cellar with a large cask on his shoulder, lurching under the weight of it. It was too dark, even with the passing of the thickest cloud from the moon, to make out his features, or anything of his dress, but she could see his shape, and that of the man who followed him out of the top gate toward the forest.

A third man emerged from the cellar. Straining to hear, Serena was sure she heard the soft thud of the door closing, but not the scrape of the key. Then they meant to come back and take the rest of the gunpowder tonight?

She watched the man adjust the heavy cask on his shoulder and then walk swiftly after his fellows. There was a decent track through the wood that led to the road. A cart could easily be driven down it.

Were the soldiers observing? Ready to follow? Or were they on foot and likely to be left behind? Her heart quickening, she wondered if she dare dress and rush out to discover…if only she could avoid being seen herself.

She stood, feeling her way to the bed side table to light the candle. And then, from outside, the unmistakable crack of a gunshot rent the air.

Chapter Ten

C OMMUNICATION BETWEEN MEMBERS of the castle patrol was clearly the problem. The next soldier Doverton and Tamar encountered had no idea of the attack on his fellow, and since he'd been watching the cliff path to the beach, he'd seen no sign of intruders coming the other way.

Leaving the injured Cobbler with him, Tamar and Doverton moved as swiftly and quietly as they could toward the other side of the castle. Suddenly, Doverton halted and flung out his arm to flatten himself and Tamar against the wall. A man walked out of the courtyard and straight past them. His elbow, crooked to steady the cask on his shoulder, almost brushed against Tamar's chest.

Unmoving, they watched him lurch along the path, past the orchard and beyond, into the wood.

Doverton began to follow at once. Tamar, torn by the desire to stay and guard the castle in general, and Serena in particular, hesitated before a faint light coming from the wood told him there were other men there, too. He loped after Doverton.

It seemed that things were finally moving. On the forest track, a cart stood in the moonlight with two casks already on it. Two men also crouched on the cart, rubbing their shoulders while the man Tamar and Doverton had been following, approached them.

Their man paused, jerking his head back toward the castle, presumably in silent instruction to bestir themselves once more and bring the rest.

Amid indistinguishable mutterings, they'd started to obey when someone leapt out of the bushes—a red-uniformed soldier, his rifle aimed somewhat shakily at the cart. "Halt in the name of the king!"

Doverton groaned. "In the name of... What in hell is he doing?"

One of these men had already pursued Serena with a knife and struck down another soldier from behind. They wouldn't hesitate to kill this one. When Doverton leapt out of the shadows, crashing through the undergrowth to join his man, Tamar was right beside him.

"Everyone halt and nobody fire!" Doverton yelled.

All heads jerked toward them. The man they were following hurled his cask onto the cart, where one man caught and steadied it. The other man on the cart leapt forward, seizing the reins and lashing the horse who lunged forward with a cry of protest, directly at the soldier who promptly dropped his rifle and bolted.

Meanwhile, the man they'd been following whipped round to face Tamar and Doverton once more. And he held a pistol. "Stop," he commanded.

By the time they skidded to a halt, there wasn't much distance between them. It might have been the lantern light, but the man's eyes seemed to glint with venomous fury, perhaps because his task had been interrupted, even in such a farcically inefficient manner.

The cart halted once more. Their man backed up to it, still holding the pistol aimed alternately at Doverton and Tamar. He eased his hip onto the cart, which was now slowly turning until the horse returned to the track. There was nothing to stop it leaving. And very little Tamar and Doverton could do to follow it on foot.

But the man with the pistol took careful aim at Doverton, and with horror, Tamar saw that he would shoot him anyway. There was nothing to lose.

Tamar hurled himself forward three paces and threw himself at the gunman. The gun seemed to explode just as he landed against the villain's body, dragging him off the cart. Doverton cried out, his words indistinguishable.

Something—a boot—struck Tamar in the chest, knocking him

away, and the cart rattled off. To his annoyance, the gunman jumped back onto the cart at the last moment.

"Bugger," he said, irritably. For some reason, it seemed to be hard to rise. His shoulder wouldn't work. "Still, at least he didn't shoot anyone."

"Idiot," Doverton fumed, crouching down beside him. "What in God's name did you do that for? He shot *you!*"

In surprise, Tamar regarded his uncooperative shoulder. He couldn't see much in the dark, now that the smugglers' lanterns had gone, but when he touched it, it was wet and sticky. "Oops."

Doverton helped haul him to his feet, and they staggered back toward the castle. The argument between them as to whether or not to seek help at the castle was taken out of their hands by a small figure who shot out of the side door Tamar already knew.

"My God, what has happened?" she cried, and Tamar smiled because it was Serena's voice.

She stood in the sudden blaze of light around her, her hair tumbling loose about her shoulders. And when he looked into her beautiful, anxious eyes, he thought that if this was the last face he ever saw, he would at least die happy.

And then the pain exploded and his world turned black.

"Is HE DEAD?" Serena whispered, stricken. Oh, he couldn't be, he just couldn't, *Please, God...*

"Not yet," Major Doverton said grimly, supporting his slumped burden. "But he's been shot and I can't see how bad it is."

"Bring him inside," Serena said at once. "I'll send to Dr. Morton—or will your soldiers be quicker?"

"Dr. Morton's in Spain," Doverton said. "We all call on Dr. Lampton now. He's reputed be good with gunshot wounds."

It took surprisingly little time to rouse the household, some of whom had already been disturbed by the shot. The stable lad was quickly dispatched on horseback for the doctor, with instructions to send him up on the same horse for quickness.

Meanwhile, two of the footmen had carried Tamar up to the nearest guest bedchamber in the main part of the castle and lit the fire in the grate, while Doverton eased off his coat and cut away his shirt.

"Well?" Serena asked shakily, holding onto the bottom bedpost for support as she glimpsed the gory wound in his shoulder.

"I'd say he's lucky," Doverton said grimly. "Looks like the ball nicked the top of his shoulder, but I don't know if it's lodged in there. I'm going to leave it to the doctor. But he'll want clean water and bandages, at the very least."

"Of course, I'll see to it," Serena said at once, hurrying off to obey. Although her instinct was to do everything for him herself immediately, she had no experience of this kind of injury, and for Tamar's sake, she had to leave this part to those who had.

Having delivered water, cloths, and bandages to the sick room, she gazed worriedly down at the patient, who was groaning as he opened his eyes. Relief at this much life flooded her, but Doverton had already piled most of her bandages onto the wound to soak up the frightening amount of blood.

Serena fled to find more, unable to shake off the fear that he would have died before she returned. She was just crossing the landing with a larger pile of bandage material when a man was admitted through the front door.

"Dr. Lampton, my lady," the footman called.

"Oh good! This way, if you please, Doctor. Thank you for coming so quickly!"

"I was up," he said shortly. "And took your horse as ordered."

Although he was still a young man, the doctor's face looked both formidable and sardonic to Serena. She could have wished for someone more sympathetic to deal with Tamar, but if he only did his job and saved the marquis's life, she would be eternally grateful.

"Your man said it was a gunshot."

"Apparently he was shot by a pistol."

The doctor curled his lip. "Another duel. I should leave the idiots to die."

Shocked, Serena stared at him as she entered the room and stood aside for him.

"Not a duel, doctor," Doverton said harshly. "This man saved my life when I was almost shot by a gang of miscreants stealing gunpowder. The pistol went off at close range when Tamar threw himself at the gunman."

Lampton shot him a quick look, then, without apology, sat on the bed and lifted the bandages from the wound. Without a word, he soaked a cloth and began cleaning it.

Serena, who was glad she couldn't see over his shoulder, gazed at Tamar's face instead. She'd always known he was a good man, a brave man. Doverton's story both warmed her with pride and terrified her.

The patient's eyes were open, shifting from the doctor's face as he twisted his head, trying to watch the doctor work.

"Be still," the doctor snapped, getting to work with his needle and thread.

Tamar obeyed, frowning instead as he gazed around the room until he found Serena. A smile broke over his face. "You. I was sure I'd seen you."

Her heart soared. She wanted to weep from sheer emotion.

"Hold that in place," the doctor instructed Doverton, and while the major held the clean cloth over the stitched wound, the doctor delved into his bag and came out with a jar.

"I've seen that evil potion before," Tamar remarked clearly.

"Yes, you have. I expected it to last me for years, short of a French invasion. Now, it's likely to be finished by Christmas."

"Sorry," Tamar said, and won a surprising if reluctant smile from the grim-faced doctor.

"Don't run in front of any more guns." Lampton slathered ointment over the wound, then bound it with swift efficiency. "You're lucky. The ball gouged out a lump of your shoulder. It nicked the bone but didn't break it, and then came out the other side. But you've lost a lot of blood. Rest here for a couple of days if they'll put up with you."

"We will," Serena said.

The doctor stood and addressed her. "If he develops a fever, send for me. Otherwise, I'll come back and change his dressing tomorrow. Some time." He nodded curtly. "Good evening."

"Thank you..." Serena gazed after him, frowning, even as she walked across to the bed.

"Don't mind him," Tamar said. "He's a good fellow...but his wife is ill, and she's carrying his child. He has worries of his own."

"How do you even know such things?" Serena demanded.

"He's a friend of mine..."

"I think he needs to sleep," Doverton said abruptly.

Serena poured a glass of water and eased him up from his pillows to drink it. He drank, yet never took his unblinking gaze off her face.

"I'm as weak as a kitten," he said.

"Good thing, too," Doverton muttered, rising to his feet. "I'll take my leave, Lady Serena—with apologies. We've made a dog's breakfast of this affair. But at least we have a theory now as to where the gunpowder's going."

"Really?" Serena said, forcing her mind to dredge up her own contribution. "They spoke in French, Major. I heard them."

Doverton didn't seem surprised. "Tamar thought they might be French, and set on breaking the prisoners-of-war out of the Black Fort."

"Using gunpowder? Is that not rather...indiscriminately dangerous?"

"It can be. It depends how much they know of the fort and how and where they plan to use the gunpowder. I'll do my best to make sure they don't get the chance to use it all."

Serena walked civilly downstairs with him, fielding questions from Maria and Miss Grey who had both been wakened by the commotion and had come to see what was going on. By the time she'd said goodbye to Major Doverton, Mrs. Gaskell the housekeeper had appeared too, as neat and tidy in her dark gown and cap as she always was.

Serena explained briefly what had happened, and that Tamar had been wounded and was now recovering in the spare bedchamber.

"Bless my soul!" Mrs. Gaskell exclaimed. "I'll sit with the poor young man until morning."

"No, Mrs. Gaskell," Serena said firmly. "You must return to your bed and get what rest you can for the rest of the night. I shall sit with Lord Tamar until morning."

"Lady Serena, it is not fitting…"

"It is perfectly fitting," Serena pronounced. "It's my fault this happened to him, and I shall be the one to see to him. You may take over in the morning, if you'd be so good."

Serena sailed past her, not prepared to brook any argument on this score. She was aware the housekeeper bridled and that Miss Grey caught her eye to advise against interference. Miss Grey, it seemed, was quite perceptive. At least her suspicion of Tamar must have been laid to rest by this night's work.

The housekeeper subsided. Serena sent everyone back to bed and returned to the sickroom.

Lord Tamar had fallen asleep, but at least he seemed to be breathing more easily than after he'd fainted. Serena touched his forehead with her palm and then the back of her hand. His skin was cool to the touch. She hadn't truly expected him to be fevered at this stage. It was an excuse to touch him.

Ashamed of herself, she went and took a spare blanket from the chest, then swung it around her shoulders and settled into the armchair beside the bed.

She woke to the pale dawn light filtering through the curtains onto her face. There was no disorientation. She knew exactly where she was, and why. Immediately, she turned her head toward the bed, and found Tamar's open eyes already upon her.

"What is it?" she asked at once. "Are you in pain?"

"No. That is, a bit, I suppose. I was just thinking how lucky a man would be to wake up every morning and see your face."

She flushed. "I don't think that's a very proper thought. Did Dr. Lampton give you laudanum?"

"Devil a bit."

She rose and went to him, letting the blanket fall back on to the chair. Only when she leaned over to touch his forehead once more did she realize her hair was still loose. She must look like a hoyden. He tilted his face, as though inhaling her scent.

Pretending not to notice, she straightened. "I don't believe you're fevered." She turned and picked up the small bottle of laudanum from the bedside table.

"No," he said, catching at her hand. "I don't want it. I like my head clear."

"Well…it's your suffering," she said doubtfully.

"I'm not suffering."

Gently, yet insistently, he drew her down until she sat on the bed facing him. "Thank you for looking after me. I promise I'll be good."

Shockingly, she wasn't sure she wanted him to be good. But since he retained her hand in his warm, strong fingers, she doubted what he meant by the word.

"Why did you do it?" she blurted.

"Get shot? I didn't *mean* to."

"Major Doverton said you threw yourself upon the pistol!"

"Well, not exactly. I think I threw myself upon the *wielder* of the pistol. I hoped to deflect his aim."

"You did," she said dryly. "And so you were shot instead of Major Doverton."

"You needn't make me sound so selfless. It was pure instinct. I just can't be responsible for taking another life." He gave a twisted smile. "My mouth is moving without permission. Perhaps I should just go back to sleep."

"Perhaps you should," she said lightly. "And keep your secrets safe."

"What secrets?" he asked. "My life is like an open book."

"Oh, I doubt that."

His lips twisted. "You want to know about my bailiff, don't you?"

"Perhaps," she admitted.

"I might tell you one day. Not today."

"Why not?" she asked anxiously. "Are you too sore?"

"No, I'm too happy." He began to sit up. "And hungry. I could eat a horse."

"I beg you won't," she said, reaching at once to help him and rearrange his pillows. "We're all very fond of our horses at Braithwaite."

He laughed, and sheer desire caught at her breath. He wore one of her brother's shirts, loosely open at the throat, and despite the visible bandage, the urge to touch his skin almost overwhelmed her.

Hastily, she straightened and slipped off the bed to sit more decorously in the armchair. The heat in his own eyes didn't vanish, but as if smoothing over any awkwardness she might feel, he began to talk. He asked her about growing up in the castle and entertained her with amusing tales from *his* childhood. Which was how she learned that his Christian name was Rupert.

"Rupert?" she repeated, intrigued. "I believe it suits you."

"No one else thinks so. I was usually called Rags."

She frowned. "Why?"

"My initials, Rupert Alan Gaunt. It suited me at school, since my clothes were always old and usually too small. My father never thought dressing his children was the best use of available funds. I believe it was Dax who made the name popular."

"Didn't you mind?"

"No, I don't think I ever did."

Before long, they were comfortably exchanging banter as they conversed, and Serena almost forgot about his injury.

They were both laughing when Mrs. Gaskell and Meg the maid came in with breakfast.

"You should go and rest, my lady," the housekeeper said repressively. "I shall take care of his lordship now."

"Actually, I don't feel tired," Serena replied, though she stood. "I dozed in the chair. But I do need to wash and change! I shall leave you in Mrs. Gaskell's capable hands, sir. Enjoy your breakfast."

ALTHOUGH IT WAS Sunday and she had intended to walk into Black-haven with the girls and go to church, she found herself reluctant to leave the patient. So were the girls. After Helen had crept in with the servant who took away his breakfast tray, it seemed pointless to keep her sisters out if Tamar was happy to be visited.

It seemed he was. In fact, he was so good-natured and entertaining that even Mrs. Gaskell warmed toward him. By the time they all ate luncheon together in his bedchamber, the atmosphere was relaxed and fun, and Tamar was chafing to be up.

Serena gave reluctant permission for him to dress and sit in the chair for an hour or two to see how he felt, and in the absence of any valet, summoned a footman to help him. Then she swept the girls out for a walk in the fresh air while the rain stayed off.

"I like Lord Tamar," Maria said as they sloshed through wet leaves at the edge of the wood.

"So do I," Alice agreed. "Much more than Sir Arthur, who barely looked at us."

Serena laughed, though it sounded a little unnatural in her ears. "Why of course he is nothing like Sir Arthur! What an odd person to compare him to."

"Is it?" Maria glanced at her. "Don't you like him?"

"Who, Lord Tamar? Of course, I like him. He's a very likeable person."

"He likes you," Helen observed.

"I hope he does," Serena managed.

"Do you think you'll marry him?" Helen asked.

Blindly, Serena shook her head. Even as all the reasons against it rushed at her—not least of them Tamar's own views—she recognized that she wanted nothing more in the world than to be his wife. A lump rose in her throat.

"We do not think of each other in that way."

Maria took her arm. "I like it when you're with him. He makes you happy."

Serena squeezed her eyes shut. "Please, don't. It isn't kind, though I know you mean well."

"He's poor," Alice pronounced.

"Very," Serena agreed.

"What does that matter?" Maria asked. "You're not."

Tell that to Braithwaite! To our mother. To Tamar himself. "Let's walk back the way," Serena said bracingly, veering from the wood back on to the path. "Until this gunpowder problem is solved, we shouldn't stray too far from the house. Besides, it's about to rain again."

As they walked across the drive toward the front of the house, they noticed a curricle and horses waiting there. A servant held the horses' heads, while a gentleman stood at the front door talking to Paton. The gentleman turned and Serena recognized the Comte de Valère.

"It's that Frenchman," Alice observed without enthusiasm. "Now he *is* like Sir Arthur."

"I don't know how you can say that when you barely met him," Serena objected. "All the same, I wonder what he wants?"

It seemed they were about to find out, for as soon as he saw them, he ran down the steps to meet them, smiling and offering his hand to Serena.

"Lady Serena, forgive the intrusion," he begged.

Serena shook hands briefly. "Of course, there is no intrusion. What might we do for you, monsieur?"

"Merely assure me of your well-being," he said at once. "I heard a soldier was attacked in the grounds last night and shots fired, and all sorts of wild rumors, so I just had to call."

"How kind of you," Serena replied. "But as you see, we are all quite unharmed." She had spent almost three seasons in London and was cynical enough to suspect he had come rather on a gossip-finding errand. She just hoped her sisters had enough common sense to keep quiet about Tamar's presence in the guest bedchamber.

"And looking as delightful as ever," Valère said, smiling and executing a bow that took in all the young ladies, before returning to Serena. "I am so relieved. What happened here last night, then?"

"We're not terribly sure," Serena said, her manner deliberately vague. "I believe Major Doverton was pursuing a particularly nasty set of smugglers."

"What a terrible business!"

"Indeed." She regarded him directly. "I'm sorry, we are not in a position to receive visitors."

"Of course, I realize that. Which is why I'm so glad to have caught you on your walk. To be frank, Lady Serena, if you could spare me just a minute more of your time, I'd also hoped to speak on another matter? A mutual friend..."

Serena presumed he meant Catherine. "Of course. We may take a turn around the front terrace. Girls, go in to Miss Grey and I'll join you in a moment."

The girls, more than happy to obey, all but bounded up the front steps and into the house.

"It's about Miss Winslow," the Comte de Valère confided as they strolled along the front of the house.

"I thought it might be."

"The trouble is, I fear I might have inadvertently raised expectations which I cannot fulfil."

Serena regarded him without favor. "In what way can they not be fulfilled?"

"Alas, while she is charming company, I do not love Miss Winslow. And I am the kind of man who can only marry for love."

"Then you should have been more careful," Serena snapped, annoyed and hurt for her friend, who had seemed to be more than half in love with the Comte.

"I know it and am sorry for it. I can only blame it on my solitude, my loneliness in this place. I am, you might say, forever a stranger."

"You were brought up here, were you not, monsieur? I can't imagine you are friendless."

"In England as a whole, of course I am not. Here in Blackhaven, I had no acquaintances. But this is no excuse. I am hoping you might explain the matter to Miss Winslow? Or give me advice as to how to let her down as gently and kindly as may be."

"I think you give yourself too much credit, sir," Serena said with coolness. "Miss Winslow will hardly go into a decline over you or any other man she barely knows."

"Of course not," he said hastily.

They had reached the end of the house, and Serena turned to walk back again. But the count remained, looking along the side of the building toward the old part of the castle. "May we walk around this way? I would love to see the original castle."

Serena hesitated between civility and irritation with him for his carelessness toward her friend's feelings. Irritation won.

"I'm afraid not today. My presence is required indoors."

"Of course," he said, offering his arm in understanding spirit.

Although Serena had no desire to take his arm, this time, civility won, and she laid her fingers lightly on his forearm. His manner was unthreatening as he placed her hand more comfortably in the crook of his elbow, only then his fingers tightened, her hand was trapped and she found herself trotting around the side of the house after all.

"Monsieur, I believe I made myself plain!" she said, outraged.

"Oh, you did, which is why I have been forced to take rather more drastic measures. In my pocket I have a dagger and a pistol. The blade, I shall use on you if you don't stop squirming. The pistol I shall use on the first of your servants stupid enough to interfere with me."

Stunned, Serena stopped trying to wrench her hand free and stared at him. Without slowing, he took his free hand from his pocket and showed her a wicked dagger that looked alarmingly well-used.

"What do you want?" she whispered.

"I want my gunpowder, which I'd never have left here if I'd guessed it would be such a damned palaver to get it out again."

"You're not an emigre at all, are you?"

"*Ma mie*, I'm not even a comte," he said contemptuously.

"You're a Bonapartist! A spy!"

"I am. Although I've never before been forced to work with such an inept set of bunglers as the fools who've been failing to remove my gunpowder from your cellar for some time now."

"They removed some of it," Serena retorted.

"Ah. I wondered if you'd noticed. It *was* you who tipped off the soldiers, then."

"Of course." She half-stumbled through the arch into the old castle courtyard. "And I'll *never* give you the cellar key!"

"If you've noticed, I've never needed your key." Releasing her squashed hand at last, he grasped her arm instead and dropped the dagger back in his pocket. "Try to run or scream or even just annoy me, and I'll cut you in pieces," he warned in amiable accents.

He produced the cellar key in one hand and whistled loudly. "Calling for my transport," he said jauntily, and unlocked the cellar door.

To her surprise and relief, he didn't pull her into the cellar but to one side of the door. His other hand grasped the dagger once more, his attitude quite incongruously casual.

The curricle came rumbling around from the front of the house, the servant trotting beside the horse. Drawing level with the door, he looped the reins through the handle and loped inside the cellar.

As his footsteps faded down the stairs, the rumbling of another vehicle reached Serena's puzzled ears. A horse and cart trotted briskly through the other arch.

The blatancy rendered Serena speechless for several seconds while the two ruffians on the box leapt down. One of them looked horribly familiar—surely the man who had threatened her with a dagger. Which seemed to be becoming a common occurrence in her life.

"You can't," Serena blurted at last. "It's broad daylight! My people will be looking for me! And if they don't stop you, the soldiers will!"

"No one will stop me," he said with a quiet confidence that was far more frightening than bluster.

"What idiocy makes you imagine that?" she demanded.

He smiled and placed the very tip of the dagger at her throat. It was only for an instant, but long enough to drive the breath from her body in fear. He said, "I have the earl's sister. And I've been in Blackhaven long enough to realize that no one will risk her. As long as I have you, I can do exactly as I wish."

Her instinct was to wrestle and scream, and indeed she did give an almost involuntary jerk, but the flash of the dagger and the memory of his other threat kept her silent and still. *The pistol I shall use on the first of your servants stupid enough to interfere with me.* She couldn't risk that. They'd already shot Tamar.

Chapter Eleven

WHILE TAMAR, WHO was interested in everyone, enjoyed getting to know the castle people, and was glad of the young ladies' company, it was Serena he wanted in the room. His shoulder ached like the fiend, but it seemed to hurt less than her absence. And she'd barely been gone two hours.

His heart lifted when the children appeared and announced that Serena would be in shortly. But he could not be still. Fully dressed now in poor Braithwaite's clothes—which weren't a bad fit and were certainly a damned sight finer than any he'd ever owned—he paced, throwing teasing remarks to the girls as they chattered.

He needed to see Serena before he left. He didn't know why. It was just necessary. As necessary as his going. That he might hurt her tore at his heart. That his absence might *not* hurt her, ate at him. All of which proved that they shouldn't ever see each other again. This, whatever this was, had already gone too far... certainly for his peace. He had to do the honorable thing and remove himself from her life.

Impatiently, he glanced out of the window, which looked onto the front of the house. He'd glimpsed the sisters walking back toward the house that way. And he was glad the visiting curricle had gone. Damned cheek, whoever it belonged to. Serena must be back in the house by now. Perhaps he should just ask one of the girls to fetch her? Or go in search of her himself? The farewell would be easier in company where he couldn't give in to any of his natural desires to take her in his arms or blurt out his feelings. Whatever they were.

He was just turning away when he heard the clop of hooves and the rumbling of wheels, and saw the damned curricle again. A well-dressed gentleman in a tall hat was driving it, and beside him sat Serena, her hands folded in her lap. But something about her posture screamed at him. This was wrong. Or perhaps he was just furious to see her with another man.

"Who is that fellow?" he demanded.

Immediately, the girls clustered around the window. Helen, at the front beside him, wrinkled her nose. "It's the Frenchman, the Comte de Valère. What is she doing with him? He's an emigre and we think he admires Serena. Only he's like Sir Arthur."

He never had time to ask in what way he was like Sir Arthur, for trailing behind the curricle came a horse and cart. And he was sure the driver and the unsavory looking men who lounged among the casks and barrels looked familiar. So did the barrels.

The blood drained from his head so fast he felt dizzy. He threw up the window, shouting something that he meant to be "Hoi!" but seemed to come out as Serena's name. Everyone below looked up at him.

Serena looked desperate and afraid. She shook her head violently. The man beside her seemed to wave in a jaunty manner, but the blade in his hand was terrifyingly clear.

"Jesus Christ," Tamar whispered and slammed the window as the men on the cart grinned up at him. Both vehicles sped off down the drive.

If ever he had to use the brains God gave him, now was the moment.

Think, you idiot!

This comte fellow was in command of the little party, and after last night, he must have known his game was rumbled, even if his identity wasn't. And so, he'd moved quickly to obtain the rest of his store.

But Tamar knew where he was going. All he had to do was get there first and pray they weren't stupid enough to harm Serena before their task was complete. He couldn't afford to think of her fear now.

"Horses," he said striding across the room and out the door. "I need horses and men."

In the entrance hallway, Mrs. Gaskell was demanding of Paton, "Where has Lady Serena gone? She said nothing to me!"

Paton opened the front door to tumultuous knocking. Jem the gardener fell into the house.

"Just the man," Tamar exclaimed, running downstairs.

"Lady Serena's gone off with some bloke in a curricle!" Jem panted. "And she doesn't want to go, I know she doesn't! And those behind have pinched the powder!"

"In a nutshell," Tamar said grimly. "Jem, can you ride?"

"I can cling on."

"Good enough for me. Get horses saddled for us and as many other men as you can find to ride them, as long as there's one horse left. Large men, preferably. Paton, I need someone to make use of that remaining horse to ride to Major Doverton with a message. It's urgent."

"What's going on?" Mrs. Gaskell cried, her hands clutching her face.

"The Comte de Valère has abducted Serena," Maria said grimly from the top of the stairs. "And stolen the gunpowder. Lord Tamar is going to get her back."

God willing. Please, God, be willing…

IT HAD BEEN several years since Serena had taken the road up to the old fort. It hadn't been raining then, and she hadn't been in an open carriage. Of course, the fort hadn't housed prisoners-of-war at that time either. Nothing much had happened there at all, despite it being the original barracks of the 44th before they'd moved into Blackhaven over a hundred years ago.

As they drove up the hill, she easily recognized the fort's distinctive castle-shape and square, crenelated tower. The horse and cart toiled up behind them.

It was an isolated spot, with only an inn about a mile further on. But any hope Serena had harbored that the prison guards would stop them, or even shoot her abductors, died as they drew nearer.

It was a prison, full of foreign inmates hated by the rest of the country. The guards were not so concerned with people approaching as with their charges trying to leave. No one watched their arrival from those crenelated towers. Or if they did, it was from glazed windows, with very little obvious interest. Only a massive, iron door guarded the outside.

The rain had gone off again by the time they arrived at the fort, but Serena was cold and wet and her hair dripped down inside the collar of her pelisse.

Valère's men seemed to know their task without instructions. Three casks were quickly unloaded at the front with one of the men, and then the cart pulled off the road. Valère urged his horses around to the back of the prison behind the cart, to the first tower which was surrounded by badly overgrown bushes and trees. But they'd been there before, she realized. They'd actually cleared a patch immediately behind the tower, large enough for the cart and the curricle to stand with ease, even for the curricle to turn so that the horse faced the fort.

When both vehicles had halted, the rest of the men jumped down and got to work. First, they kicked aside the brush they must have laid down earlier to keep the ground dry, and gave the horses something to crop to keep them still and content. Then, they unloaded the barrels and casks from the cart, and pulled more out of their hiding places in the bushes. They set about laying trails and fuses. Even Valère was so busy, she thought she could walk away without him even noticing.

"This is madness," she told him urgently. "You'll probably kill half the inmates. And what if some do get out? It's only a matter of time until they're recaptured. They can't all have the means to pretend to be emigrés like you!"

"Thank God I won't have to pretend much longer," he returned, prying the top of another barrel.

"You'll end up in there with the rest," she taunted, waving one disparaging hand at the tower.

"No, I shall end up on a French ship currently waiting five miles down the coast from Blackhaven. And I believe I will take you with me for company."

"Oh dear," she flashed back. "Are you lonely in France, too?"

He gave a snort that might actually have been laughter, and she, appalled that he might imagine some rapport between them, looked away in disgust. Which is when she glimpsed the movement in the overgrown bushes beside her.

Instantly, her heart began to beat with hope, but, afraid of drawing attention to what she'd seen, she glanced back at Valère and the men, busy about their work. Testing her theory, she stood, meaning to jump down from the curricle on the side farthest away from the prison walls. They'd catch her again, of course, but it would slow things up, perhaps provide time for whoever observed from the bushes, to warn the prison guards what was going on.

"Do not," Valère commanded. "Even if my dagger misses you, my men will catch you in under four seconds. They are not gentle like me."

"A dagger is gentle in your world?" she retorted, subsiding back into the seat but casting a quick glance into the bushes. A hand emerged, and then a head. Her eyes widened impossibly, for it was Tamar.

Tamar was wounded! He should be sitting quietly in his chamber if not resting in his bed. How in God's name...?

And so, her agony changed, from worrying about how to prevent this, to worrying about Tamar. Valère and the others had the will and the means to kill without compunction.

"Stop, now," she commanded the Frenchmen. "I'll scream and sing to warn them inside."

"Sing away," Valère said carelessly. "It's too late to stop this now, whichever way they come."

"Wrong." Tamar said, erupting from the bushes, four other men at his heels. Jem was among them, and John the head groom. But she had no time to count heads, for quick as a flash, Valère was responding to the attack with his pistol, aiming it straight at the rushing Tamar. It seemed he'd forgotten his promise to use the knife first on Serena.

Or perhaps she was just too valuable in his escape plan. Either way, she was the only one who could stop him before he fired.

"Geddup!" she yelled, seizing the reins and lashing the horses. Screaming their annoyance, they bolted directly at Valère, not only blocking his aim but forcing him back. He stumbled into the wall as Serena wrenched the horses' heads around, and then Tamar was on him, ramming his head and his wrist into the wall.

She saw no more, for she'd flashed past them, crashing around the prison toward the road. It seemed Tamar and his allies were unaware of the explosives at the front door. And as the horses hit the road, she pulled them around again, charging straight at the Frenchman who was about to light the fuse.

He leapt, trying in vain to escape the flying hooves that kicked him and the taper across the street.

With a sob, Serena strove to slow and calm the horses she'd so deliberately riled, gentling them until they finally came to a halt. Only then did she coax them into turning. Fortunately, there was a wide stretch of grass, with no ditch between it and the road. Even so, her hands shook so much, she was vaguely surprised she didn't overturn the curricle as they circled around and trotted in a civilized fashion back to the fort.

By then, prison guards had erupted from the iron door, gunpowder was being swept up, and a whole troop of soldiers from the 44th had appeared. Bizarrely, so had a closed carriage and Kate Grant, who was running to meet her.

Serena halted the curricle, sliding down unaided into Kate's arms, while a soldier held the horses' heads.

"Tamar?" she gasped to Kate. "Where is Tamar?"

Kate turned toward the side path, and Serena saw Tamar on horseback, white-faced but determined, the reins held in one hand while the other hung useless at his side. His shoulder must have been in agony.

"I think he's looking for you," Kate drawled.

Her eyes clashed with Tamar's. The flooding relief in his face almost undid her.

Kate swallowed. She was afraid of crying. "Is he…is he?" she began brokenly.

"I think he's fine," Kate said brusquely. "Come, in you go. I'll be with you in one moment and take you home."

Serena, her vision blurring, found herself led to the closed carriage in which, presumably, Kate had travelled here. Then she was seated against the comfortable squabs, and the door was closed. She breathed in long, panting breaths.

Abruptly, the door flew open again. Tamar leapt in, slamming it shut behind him. Even before he'd thrown himself onto the seat beside her, her arms were reaching for him, and then at last she clutched him to her.

His arms wrapped around her, holding her close. "Serena," he whispered into her hair. "Are you hurt?"

"No, I'm fine," she said impatiently. "But you, your wound…"

"It's a damned scratch, it's nothing. Serena—" His hands in her hair, he pulled back her head and crushed her mouth under his in a fierce, desperate kiss.

Her lips fell open for him at once, kissing him back with all her fear and love and joy. Tears spilled unchecked down her cheeks and into their mouths. She could taste them.

"Please don't cry," he whispered against her lips. "Please, never cry, and certainly not for me. You'll never know how much I love you."

With a sob of amazed gladness, she kissed him again. She felt the rough, tender pressure of his mouth for an instant more, and then he tore himself free.

"Goodbye," he said incoherently.

The door opened, letting him jump down, and slammed again, leaving her stunned in the corner, wondering what had just happened.

She didn't know if she was laughing or crying when Kate was handed in and the carriage began to move, taking her home to Braithwaite Castle.

"WHAT ARE YOU doing here?" Serena asked as the carriage bumped down the road toward Blackhaven. "How did you know?"

"Well, there were rumors flying in church this morning, about shots fired in the castle grounds, and a soldier killed—"

"I don't believe he was killed," Serena corrected. "But he was hurt."

"At any rate, Tristram sent me to see that you were all well, and I drove up in the carriage, being lazy and disinclined to get wet. Mrs. Gaskell told me what had happened—and I must admit I would never have thought such a thing of Valère. He seemed the perfect gentleman. Except for the way he treated Catherine, of course."

"I think she was his excuse to linger longer in Blackhaven if he needed to," Serena said, wrinkling her nose. "But our arrival at the castle forced them to rush. I gather from their conversation that they originally meant to blow up the walls at night, with their prisoners well informed and a ship waiting in Braithwaite Cove. But they hadn't moved all the gunpowder by the time we arrived, and then, of course, I found it. After last night, they knew they were rumbled. How did you know to come to the fort?"

"Maria told me. She'd heard you and Doverton discussing it, apparently. I only just stopped her climbing into the carriage with me."

"Thank you for that, but it was ridiculously brave of you to come at all!"

"Not in the slightest," Kate drawled. "Mere curiosity, I assure you. And I gathered I was likely to be safe, after my carriage fell in with Major Doverton on his way up here. By then, of course, Tamar and your people had disarmed both villains and the gunpowder. And you had spectacularly mown down the man Tamar had lost track of, saving, I understand, the fort door and the two guards lounging just inside it."

"I didn't think I could do it. Did I hurt him really badly?"

Kate shrugged. "He'll live. Though you seemed to give him a spectacular fright."

"That, he deserves."

"Well, Major Doverton has given them all into custody at the fort for now. I expect they'll be taken to London though, and probably hanged as spies, in the end."

Serena shivered. "It's time this war ended, isn't it?"

"I believe Bonaparte is almost beaten. They say he can't recover now. It's just a matter of time."

"And more lives."

Kate regarded her with interest. "As you say. But you saved many today, you and Tamar and the others. You should be proud."

Serena swallowed. "Thank you."

There was a pause. "Tamar was distraught when he heard you'd bolted in the curricle. Almost as distraught as you were about him when you arrived back."

Serena dropped her gaze. Kate was too perceptive for comfort.

"I like Tamar," she said. "Everyone likes him. But you know, through no fault of his own, he has a mountain of debt and not even two pennies to rub together."

"I know." *It doesn't matter. I have.*

"I wish you all the best," Kate said, with just a hint of pity. "But if you truly wish this, you'll have to fight Braithwaite and your mother."

"I know. But I'll be twenty-one in a few months." She could hold out until then. She could do anything for Tamar.

"You love him," Kate said quietly.

Serena's heart soared. There was intense new pleasure as well as pride in admitting it. "Yes, I love him."

Chapter Twelve

ONE OF THE hardest things Tamar had ever done was ride straight past Braithwaite Castle that afternoon and carry on to Blackhaven.

His shoulder ached, and blood was seeping out from the bandages, staining Braithwaite's white shirt. Exhausted and slightly dizzy, he needed to lie down. After he'd seen Lampton, and before he dealt with Julian.

Doverton, clearly worried, rode with him to the doctor's house and promised to look after the borrowed horse.

Tamar fully expected the rough side of the doctor's occasionally blistering tongue, but to his surprise, Lampton looked almost pleased to see him. In silence, he took him into his study, sat him down, cleaned and re-stitched the wound before covering it with a clean dressing.

"Don't do it again," he said, helping Tamar ease his shirt and coat back on. It was almost the first thing he'd said. The man clearly had agonies of his own that put Tamar's firmly in perspective.

Lampton's expected loss was beyond words. Tamar laid a hand on his shoulder for an instant and then left. It was all he could do.

When he arrived at his front door, at least Rivers was not there. Which was good. Probably. Perhaps he'd finally given up.

Inside, he stumbled his way through the darkness and flopped onto his couch, fully dressed.

When he woke, it was still dark, but he had no idea of the time. Ignoring the protest of his wound, he struggled to his feet, fumbled his way to the tinder box, and lit the candle. Then he peered out of his window, and to his relief, saw by the moon that he'd only been asleep for a couple of hours. His stomach rumbled. At least he'd find supper at the club.

Fortunately, there was still clean water in the jug. He washed and tidied up his clothes—Braithwaite's clothes—suspecting he still looked smarter than he usually did, then dragged a brush through his hair and left the cottage.

Since he'd invited Linnet to come with him, and still wanted the excuse of her presence to be there, he walked round to her rooms, prepared to find her gone out already. But she seemed delighted to see him.

"I thought you'd forgotten," she admitted, wrapping a silk shawl around her pretty shoulders. She did look beautiful, enough reason to lure any man to a gambling den.

He offered his arm, and she took it, smiling. She seemed genuinely happy to be on the arm of a man with nothing but debt. He wished Linnet a good husband. Or at the very least, a good protector.

Once or twice a month, the hotel held a gaming club in its large, back hall. They billed it as exclusive, though in fact, every card sharp and loose screw in the county made an appearance, along with a few more from further afield. Inevitably, his friend Dax had played here, and started a fight from all accounts, For Tamar, who avoided gaming as a rule, this was new territory.

"*Is* the play fair?" he asked Linnet as they walked up to the hotel.

"Oh, they'll skin you alive and blackball you for cheating," Linnet replied. "If they catch you."

"Excellent."

"What *are* you up to?"

"Private business," he replied. "But if it works out, I can at least repay you by taking you for supper."

As they crossed the hotel foyer, a vulgarly glittering female who laughed too loudly sailed through the double doors to the club room. An instant of smoke and noise was cut off again as the door closed behind her and her shifty looking escort. Tamar supposed the hotel must make a lot of money from these events, because they were certainly in danger of lowering the tone of the whole establishment.

He paused at the reception desk. "I don't suppose you have a Mr. Sylvester staying here, do you?"

"No, my lord," the young clerk replied at once. "No one of that name."

It was the same answer he'd received before from a different clerk. And it bore out what Tamar already suspected, that Julian had laid the trail for him at the tavern and never meant to be found here. He, more than anyone, knew that Tamar avoided gaming dens. He really expected to get away with this, and as a bonus, probably thought Sylvester would get the blame, too.

Although Tamar had paid no subscription, no one stopped him entering the hall at the back. Being a marquis, and an instantly recognizable one at that, clearly still had some advantages.

The club gave an initial impression of superiority. The furnishings were tasteful and clean, the room bright from the central chandelier and a blaze of candles spread all around. Among the clientele were several noblemen and lesser gentlemen, but at closer glance, the ladies present, although many were richly dressed and bejeweled, were no ladies, but actresses, opera dancers, and courtesans. And among them, no doubt, a few flim-flammers and those more blatantly determined to part a man from his money before he lost it all at the gaming tables.

In just such places had Tamar's father squandered his fortune, his estate, and the future of his children. If Tamar ever managed to fix the estate, he'd make damned sure to get himself several heirs, because if Julian ever inherited, he'd do exactly the same as the old marquis.

Tamar strolled around with Linnet on his arm, taking in the tables and the players, until he found the supper table, already set out with cold dishes. He and Linnet refreshed themselves with a little nourishment and a glass of wine, while Tamar finally located his brother.

Lord Julian Gaunt sat at what was clearly the high stakes table, playing with a wealthy old nobleman, and several men Tamar didn't know. He did, however, recognize the type. None of them would take well to being cheated. And it was quite clear to Tamar that Julian was cheating. He had to be; he was winning. And he had no idea that Tamar was present. Time to introduce himself.

"What would you like to play?" he asked Linnet as they strolled in that direction.

"Well, not there, anyhow!" Linnet paused beside Julian's table of intent players. "Too rich for my blood."

"But not, apparently for mine," Tamar observed, without lowering his voice.

Julian's gaze flew from up from the cards, his face whitening in appalled recognition.

Tamar smiled. "Julian," he said affectionately. "What a pleasure."

SERENA, WITH HER escort of triumphant stable lads, gardeners, and farm hands, had come home to a tumultuous and emotional welcome. She'd strained at the window for most of the journey, fearing for Tamar's hurts and wanting to stop and take him into the carriage. Kate had said only that Doverton would look after him.

When she finally stepped out of the carriage and into the arms of her sisters, she realized that neither Doverton nor Tamar were among her escort. And she couldn't ask, not in public. Instead, she formally thanked her heroic escort for coming to her aid and recklessly promised them extra ale, a day's holiday, and a bonus in their next wages. For which she was cheered all over again.

As she finally went inside, she heard Paton giving them another speech, about how they had to keep their mouths shut about this whole event. If the truth came out, right or wrong, Serena's reputation could be damaged.

For the same reason, Mrs. Gaskell and Kate between them decided it would be best for Kate to dine at the vicarage that night.

"Well, it will either be good for me, or bad for you and Mr.

Grant," Serena said sardonically when she and Kate had a moment to themselves. "What a lot of nonsense so-called propriety is!"

"It *is* nonsense," Kate agreed. "On the other hand, it can genuinely hurt you. I should know. Blackhaven chose to receive me in the end, but if I'd chosen to return to London, things might not have gone so well for me."

"Do you miss it? London?" Serena asked curiously.

"No. It still surprises me sometimes. But if I wasn't born to be a vicar's wife, I was clearly meant to be this vicar's wife."

"It's love that makes the difference," Serena said, gazing out of the window. "They never tell you that when they teach you accomplishments for catching a suitable husband."

"No, they don't," Kate agreed. "Come, fetch your bonnet and let's make haste to Blackhaven. Tristram will want his dinner after the evening service."

Dinner at the vicarage was a pleasant affair, and if Serena was inclined to dream, her hosts chose not to remark upon it. Kate regaled her husband with the day's adventures, which he knew nothing of, although it was already being whispered that Major Doverton had arrested several French spies, and the Comte de Valère's name was being whispered in shocked tones.

"Poor Catherine," Kate said ruefully. "We must keep her busy and entertained over the next few weeks."

"Indeed, we must," Serena said. "I almost wish Mama were here so that we could hold a party at the castle. Mr. Grant, have you heard no word of Lord Tamar?"

"No, but if he knocked himself up again fighting, he probably called on Dr. Lampton. I'll be calling there myself later, so I may be able to reassure you."

After dinner, Mr. Grant offered to escort them for an evening walk. And so, they strolled along the harbor and walked back via the high street, where they amused themselves glancing in shop windows to admire or disparage. In Mrs. Drake's millinery, Kate found an absolutely ridiculous hat that she insisted she would buy the very next day.

"It would certainly keep your friends in good spirits," Mr. Grant remarked.

"I'm sure I could carry it off."

"As a figure of fun," Serena said dryly. "Anyone would be." She turned away from the window and only a few yards away saw Lord Tamar vanishing through the front door of the hotel. "Oh no. I was hoping he would be abed and asleep, by now."

"Well, he is a grown man," Kate said, "and may be as silly as he wishes."

Serena knew it. Nor did she have either the right or the inclination to tell him off. But the urge to see him, to assure herself of his wellbeing, just to hear his voice, suddenly overwhelmed her.

"Do you think we might have a last cup of tea or coffee in the hotel?" she blurted. "It would surely be quite proper when you are both with me."

Kate glanced uncertainly at her husband, who smiled faintly. "Under normal circumstances I'm sure it would be. However, tonight is one of the gaming club nights, and those are not proper at all. Not for ladies. Are they, Kate?"

Kate smiled back with suspicious innocence. "Not in the slightest. Although it is my belief, Lord Tamar is no gambler."

"No," Grant agreed. "Nor does he have the money to be, not here."

"Then he is probably looking for a cup of coffee." Serena walked determinedly up to the door. "Like us."

Her heart beat quickened as she walked into the hotel and into the quiet dining room. A few people were enjoying a late supper at a table in the window, but otherwise, the place was quiet. Of Tamar, there was no sign. Her heart slowed again, sinking with disappointment.

Mr. Grant saw the ladies seated in the coffee room, then ordered refreshment before strolling back out.

"He must be visiting someone," Serena said. Truly, it was none of her business.

Kate nodded. "He is acquainted with just about everyone in Black-haven."

Although there was no reason for it, a sense of foreboding began to close in on Serena, as if something bad, something tragic were about to happen. And yet, she couldn't just walk out and let it happen without her. Because Tamar was there and her poor, obsessed heart wanted just another glimpse of him.

JULIAN RECOVERED QUICKLY. There was that much in his favor.

"Tamar," he said, playing his cards. "Come to disapprove or pit your skills against mine?"

"A bit of both, actually. Good luck." And he strolled on with Linnet, until she found a game she wished to join.

He watched her for a little, and then wandered back to watch Julian. Who was being careful. He didn't win every hand. But the pile of winnings at his elbow had grown even in the short time since Tamar had last seen it.

"Damn it, you have the devil's own luck!" the old aristocrat on his left said in disgust, throwing down another lost hand.

Of course, luck had nothing to do with it. Tamar could see exactly what Julian was doing. Julian noticed him immediately this time, although he pretended not to. Tamar strolled around the table, among the other interested observers, until he came to stand behind Julian's chair.

Julian shifted, as if he wanted to elbow him away. But of course, he couldn't. Tamar waited patiently until his brother was ready to slide the hidden card from his sleeve into his hand, and then clapped him heavily on the shoulder.

"Good to see you winning for a change," he said amiably.

Julian jumped, not just because of the fright, but because he half-expected discovery to follow immediately. And even when it didn't, he recognized that his brother's words had just informed everyone that

Julian usually lost, thus sewing a grain of suspicion in the minds of those prone to doubts. He couldn't help glancing up irritably at Tamar.

"You're distracting me," he said coldly.

"I mean to." Tamar smiled with even greater frost. "Collecting my debt before you spend your winnings." He put out his hand toward Julian's pile of notes and coins, and at once, Julian slapped his own hand over it, protective and aggressive.

Tamar let his smile broaden, while he looked directly into his brother's eyes and tapped him admonishingly on the cuff, almost exactly over the place he hid cards. There was one there now, he could feel it under his fingertips.

"Really?" Tamar said softly.

"This fellow owe you, Tamar?" the old gentleman asked. "Don't mind taking a break while he pays you." He hoped, no doubt, that the break would change his luck. It might, though hardly for the reasons he imagined.

"He does," Tamar confirmed. "Don't you, Julian? And we always pay. In full."

His meaning was clear, and Julian saw it right away. He had to pay up everything, including the pictures he still held, or Tamar would reveal the cards hidden on his person. From the hard faces at this table, they wouldn't treat cheats lightly. The may have come to fleece the unsuspecting themselves, but being fleeced in return was quite unpalatable.

"Damn it, Tamar, later is better. I have to run with the luck."

"It's about to change," Tamar said flatly.

Julian snatched up his hand with fury, and Tamar swiftly scooped up the winning. "Come, let us settle up," he said cheerfully and led the way to the door, leaving Julian no choice but to follow his money.

Trotting after him toward the reception desk. Julian snarled, "Rupert, give me the damned money or I'll—."

"Or you'll what, Julian?" He smiled at the clerk at the desk. "My brother is leaving early tomorrow morning and would like to settle his account now."

"No, I bloody wouldn't!"

"Yes, you bloody would. Or you can walk back in there and I'll shake all the cards out of you."

Perfectly wooden-faced, the clerk presented the account on the desk, somewhere between the two men.

Tamar whistled. "You like to live well, eh, Julian?" He emptied the card winnings on the desk and counted out the reckoning, adding a little extra. "And the room key, if you please."

Julian's face went from angry to ugly. "Far enough, Tamar, you have no right to—"

"No right?" Tamar repeated. He actually laughed. "You're here with my money and I want it back. We can call the Watch if you like, but…"

"Damn you," Julian said between his teeth.

Tamar scooped up the remaining money with the key. "Lead on." He whirled around toward the stairs, and that was when he saw Serena and the Grants at the dining room door. They must have heard everything. The world tilted and righted itself.

It didn't matter, nothing mattered since she couldn't be his. She might as well see the full awfulness she was avoiding.

He gave an ironic bow, then followed Julian upstairs, ready to dodge any backward kicks his brother might aim at him in order to avoid these losses.

The pictures were easily located, propped up inside the wardrobe in Julian's chamber. As far as Tamar could remember, they were all there, including Daxton's portrait.

"How did you find me?" Julian asked.

"I know you," Tamar said shortly. He glanced up from the bed where he'd piled the paintings. "Did Rivers help you?"

"He thought it was funny."

In spite of everything, it still hurt. Julian knew what Rivers was. But he hid that pain along with all the others. "I'm sure you both found it absolutely hilarious. You didn't even pay him, did you?"

"No, though he thinks I will."

"Don't," Tamar said, wrapping up the pictures together. "From now on, he gets nothing from any of us."

Julian blinked. "And if he tells?"

"Then I'll stand trial for murder. Who knows, Julian? You might get to be marquis after all. I wish you joy of it. There's certainly no fortune in it." He paused, then took out one of the seascapes and threw it back on the bed before picking up the others. "See what you can get for that."

Julian frowned. "You're giving me one? Why?"

Tamar shrugged. "You showed me I could get more for them. Call it your reward. There won't be another. Be on the stagecoach tomorrow." And he left, what was left of the money in his pocket and his pictures under his good arm.

He supposed it had been a good day. It just felt like a bad one because there would no Serena at the end of it.

Serena... As he ran downstairs, he wondered what the devil she'd been doing here at the hotel. Was she looking for him?

He'd almost forgotten about Linnet, who rushed at him from the bottom of the stairs with great glee. "That man owed you money and you got it back! Everyone's thrilled for you, and so am I!" To prove it, she flung both arms around his neck and kissed him full on the mouth.

"Well, for that, I'll take you to supper," he said, laughing as he placed her hand more decorously on his arm. Only then did he see across the foyer to the sofa where Serena sat with the Grants on either side of her. She looked...stricken.

Tamar felt sick. She must have been waiting for him, to make sure of his wellbeing. He didn't want her to be hurt. He didn't want to do the hurting, but there was no way out of this. He was so unsuitable it was laughable. And she might as well know it.

There was nothing for it now. With Linnet on his arm he crossed the hall and paused to bow. "Ladies. Grant."

Grant nodded. "I see you got your pictures back."

"I did."

Serena rose to her feet. "Congratulations," she said in a curiously hard voice that almost broke his heart. "Now there is just your bailiff to deal with and your life will be rosy. Goodbye, Lord Tamar."

In spite of everything, it was the goodbye that did it. Because she'd been hurt by the wrong thing. Although Linnet's presence here was innocent, she would not consider that, any more than she seemed to consider the obvious things of which he was guilty—poverty, failure to bring up his siblings decently, murder...

But, of course, she didn't know about that. Yet.

Through the haze of pain and anger, he saw her walking away, following Kate toward the front door.

"One moment," he said to Linnet and hurried after them. He caught her almost at the front door, planting himself squarely in front of her, separating her from Kate and Grant. "Why do you look at me like that? I'm no different from this afternoon."

"No. I just see that you have not been truthful. Friends should at least be truthful."

"Yes, they should," he snapped back. "So, here's the truth about the damned bailiff. His name is John Rivers and he really is a bailiff. It's a family firm. But, of course, he doesn't dun me for debts. For years I've paid him to keep quiet about a crime I committed."

Her eyes widened with bewilderment. "What crime?" she asked.

"Murder," he said with relish, and walked back to Linnet.

Chapter Thirteen

L ORD BRAITHWAITE HAD barely risen from his bed, had not even approached the crucial matter of his cravat, when his servant informed him that his lady mother wished to see him in the breakfast room.

The earl, being a well-mannered and tolerant man, did not groan. But he had his mind on the important speech he was to give in the House of Lords today and he really did not wish to be distracted by whatever trivialities his mother deemed important today.

However, she *was* his mother. And she never gave up. So, he tied his cravat in haste, allowed his valet to help him into his coat, and went downstairs to the breakfast room.

"Where is the fire, Mother?" he inquired flippantly, seating himself beside her at the table and pouring himself a cup of coffee.

"Nowhere, yet," she snapped. "It is what I'm trying to avoid. We went the wrong way to work with your sister. We shouldn't have sent her away."

Braithwaite, who had said so at the time, refrained from comment.

His mother picked up a letter she had been reading. "I received this from Kate Crowmore, who for reasons best known to herself, married the new vicar of Blackhaven."

"I know," Braithwaite said mildly. "He seems to be an excellent fellow. I like him."

"Well, that is nothing to the purpose." The countess waved the vicar aside. "Kate has asked my permission to relax the constrictions we placed upon her, and chaperone her to the Assembly Room ball and a few other events in Blackhaven. Using her own experience, she surmises that without respectable distraction, Serena will no doubt make her own, which should be a terrifying prospect for all of us."

"She's joking," Braithwaite observed.

"Well, of course she is. It's her way, so as not to give us offence, but she does speak the truth. We were too harsh with Serena."

Braithwaite shrugged. "I was angry. So were you. Write to her as well as to Kate, and give permission for her to enjoy herself."

"No, I think we must go there. Immediately."

"Well, if you feel you must," Braithwaite said.

"*We.* I said *we.* We may leave before midday and—"

"I can't go anywhere today," Braithwaite said firmly. "I have commitments. To be frank, I don't see why you have to go either. A letter will suffice."

His mother shook her head stubbornly. "No, I need to see Serena. I know she said she was relieved to be no longer engaged, and I believe it's true, but her mood was…strange. I believe part of her was hurt, and our reaction of immediately sending her away truly does make her ripe for mischief. I believe she needs me and I require your escort."

"I'm sorry to disoblige you," Braithwaite said with as much patience as he could muster, "but I cannot go today."

His mother frowned and shifted with annoyance in her chair. "I will wait until tomorrow then, but no longer!"

"WHERE IS LORD Tamar?" Helen demanded, in the middle of her lessons.

"I don't know," replied Serena, who had taken to disrupting her sisters' lessons once more. It had been two days since her abduction and she was more restless than ever.

"He said he would paint us," Helen said accusingly. "Why don't you send him a note to remind him? After all, you like him, too."

I did, but he's not the man I thought he was. The vision of the unknown woman kissing him with such familiarity kept repeating in her mind. That and his face, unaccustomedly harsh and brutal. *Murder.*

Maybe, she kept them deliberately in her mind to make herself grateful for his absence, to stop herself missing him. It didn't work.

"We could walk down to Blackhaven this afternoon," Alice suggested. "We could call it an art lesson, Miss Grey!"

"Oh, yes, do let's," Helen agreed with enthusiasm.

"Right now, you must return to your numbers," Miss Grey ordered, fixing Serena with her gaze.

Serena gave a faint, apologetic smile. "I'm sorry," she murmured, and slipped out of the school room.

A few minutes later, she found herself in the drawing room, sitting by the pianoforte with her fingers spread over the keys. She'd done all this before, on the day she'd first seen Tamar striding across the garden.

She couldn't help turning her head, but she could see no one at all, let alone a tall, disheveled figure burdened by an easel and a battered satchel. She couldn't understand why being so wrong about him hurt so much. Perhaps because at heart she didn't really believe it. She just knew he was pushing her away, abandoning her. The reasons, true or not, seemed to take second place in her confused mind.

What kind of immoral fool does that make me? she wondered, pressing on the keys to see what sort of a sound they made. Discordant. She didn't care about his poverty, or his womanizing, or even his crime. She cared that he wasn't here.

Unbearable thought. Hastily, to make herself think of anything other than him, she began to play. It began badly, loudly, but as the music came back to her, she played as it was meant to be, and was still playing when Mrs. Grant was announced.

"Goodness," Kate said. "You're a lot better than I ever was."

Serena smiled faintly. "I doubt that. I'm certainly a lot worse than when I was nagged to practice." She closed the lid and stood up to ring for tea.

Kate came closer, examining her with calm perception. They

hadn't seen each other since Sunday night at the hotel.

"You're looking pale and wan," Kate observed. "Are you ill?"

"Not at all. I suppose I haven't slept well since Sunday. Wretched spies."

"Or wretched marquis?" Kate suggested shrewdly.

Serena laughed. It sounded unnaturally brittle. "Of course not. I haven't forgotten he saved me on Sunday."

"You haven't forgotten he was with another woman on Sunday either."

Impatiently, Serena waved that way, but Kate wouldn't let it rest.

"Everyone knows Tamar doesn't gamble," she observed. "I daresay he needed someone to give him an excuse to be there."

"You're quite mistaken if you imagine I care about such things."

"Am I?" Kate said with deliberation.

Serena looked away.

"Well, I have come to talk to you about other things," Kate said at last. "Namely, entertaining Catherine."

Serena brightened. "I sent her a note suggesting she meet us for an ice and a visit to the circulating library. If I can prevail upon Miss Grey, I'll bring the girls—they tend to distract people! And I thought a moonlight revel on the beach might be something a little out of the ordinary."

"And cold at this time of year!"

"And possibly wet at any time of year."

"Not insurmountable problems, though," Kate said thoughtfully. "It will take some planning, so we could even get Catherine to help."

"That's what I thought. And we will need all the old biddies to pronounce it respectable, so Mrs. Winslow's support would be useful."

"Well thought out," Kate approved. "All I could think of was a theatre party! Which I have arranged, at least and shall write to Mrs. Winslow this afternoon. Oh, and Mrs. Penhalligan is to hold a rout next week."

"Who is Mrs. Penhalligan?" Serena asked, dredging her memory.

"A widow. She came here for her health after her husband died—

on the Peninsula, I believe—and liked the town so much she bought a house here. She has a son of about Bernard Muir's age and two daughters, who are now trying to drag her out of mourning. They had persuaded her to hold a small party and invite their friends, but I have worked on her to expand it!"

Kate wiggled her eyebrows in a theatrically wicked manner, and Serena couldn't help smiling.

"You are ingenious," Serena approved.

"I am. You should receive an invitation today. I assured her you were very condescending."

Kate wrinkled her nose. "Does she think I am some great lady? She's going to be disappointed—or perhaps just relieved!"

"Well, you are the greatest lady currently in Blackhaven, and the town reveres your family."

Serena sighed as the tea tray was finally brought in. "Speaking of my family, I'm not really obeying the strictures of mine, am I?"

"Well, I did write to your mother. And if you don't receive a furious letter in the next day or so forbidding you, I think you might consider it consent."

"With Wicked Kate as my chaperone?"

Kate looked unnaturally prim. "My dear, I am no longer wicked. I am the vicar's wife. Oh, and speaking of the vicar, he does have duties, so we can't make him escort us to everything. I thought we might prevail upon Bernard Muir."

"Truly?" Serena said doubtfully. "Doesn't he admire you excessively?"

"Oh, that was months ago. Now he is in love with a mill owner's daughter who is also a fabulous heiress and that is lasting much longer. Unfortunately, her parents don't like the match."

Serena bridled on her old friend's behalf. "What is wrong with Bernard?"

"He doesn't have a title. They think because the girl is so rich and so beautiful, they may look as high as they like for a husband."

"They should talk to Lord Tamar," Serena said brutally. "It would be his perfect solution."

"I daresay the girl would come around. She is quite malleable, and Tamar is handsome and good natured. Would you really wish them well?"

Serena looked away. "I am angry with him. But I do not wish him ill."

"My dear, you are more than angry." Kate nudged her arm. "I don't like to see you so down. I heard what he said to you, but truly you don't know the circumstances or even if he meant it literally—"

"I don't care if he meant it literally," Serena all but snapped.

"Then it is the actress. All men have women in their past."

Serena cast her a glance that Kate read easily enough.

"According to Tristram," Kate said, "she accompanied him to the club to give him an excuse to be there. Everyone knows Tamar doesn't gamble."

"I don't care about her either," Serena said, pushing her teacup across the table and rising to her feet.

"Then what?" Kate demanded. "Because you cannot pretend to *me* that you suddenly don't care for him."

"But I don't. He isn't who I thought he was. Don't you see, Kate? He found it too *easy* to push me away and be back in her arms—if he ever left them—the very same day! I read too much into a silly flirtation. I hate him because *I* was fooled!"

Kate searched her face. "Do you?"

"Yes." Serena turned away, walking to the window. "And I saw it in his eyes. He was *trying* to push me away, to hurt me, in order to make me leave him alone. Let it be, Kate, I have some pride. Did you come in the carriage or walk?"

Kate permitted the change of subject. "I walked since the weather is fine."

"Then we shall accompany you back to Blackhaven. The girls have decided Miss Grey looks peaky, so we are all going to make her drink the waters."

Miss Grey permitted lessons to finish early, but by the time they

reached the Pump Room, Serena had the impression that the governess had merely been the girls' excuse. It was Serena they truly wished
to drink the waters.

"Are you involved in this conspiracy?" Serena asked Miss Grey as
they left. She felt rather full of water and sat down on the bench
opposite, in a blink of autumnal sunshine.

The girls were kindly rushing in and out of the building, refilling
glasses of water for old and infirm people who wished to enjoy the
fresh air, too.

"Well, I agreed they could pretend I was a little under the weather," Miss Grey confessed. "They're really worried about you and don't
want you to know. They are sweet-natured girls."

"They are," Serena said, touched. "But truly, I am not ill."

"But you are a little blue-devilled," Miss Grey observed.

Serena would have denied it, except the girls suddenly flew across
from the Pump Room, calling, "Lord Tamar!"

Serena's stomach gave an unpleasant jolt, for the familiar tall,
rumpled figure of the marquis was loping up the steps from the beach
below. It was too late to stop her sisters from talking to him, so she
had to be content with not looking. She turned her accusing gaze upon
Miss Grey instead.

"Is this part of your conspiracy, too?"

"No," Miss Grey replied with a hint of nervousness. "But since the
subject has come up, I did want to say… I hope you have not dwelled
too much on the suspicions I once shared with you? Concerning his
lordship's involvement with the smugglers who turned out to be spies.
Because subsequent events obviously proved me utterly wrong."

"Of course not," Serena said.

The girls were walking with Tamar, chattering away to him as
they always did. He had to come this way to return to the center of the
town and as he drew closer, Serena saw that he looked as he always
did. Except, perhaps for a little pallor, no doubt caused by the loss of
blood from his wound. He wore his disreputable satchel over his other
shoulder, the uninjured one. Serena swallowed. She could not afford

to worry about his health. He was clearly well enough.

His banter with the girls might have been a little distracted, but that was normal for him, too. The ache of loss intensified. But no one could ever know.

"Look, Serena, we have found Lord Tamar," Helen cried.

"So I see. What a happy chance for him," she said wryly, and the girls laughed.

Lord Tamar bowed in his casual manner. "Lady Serena. Miss Grey."

"Good afternoon," Serena said distantly.

"Come and have tea with us at the hotel," Maria invited.

Appalled, Serena could do more than frown at her.

But Tamar was shaking his head. "Another time, I would love to. Sadly, I need to be elsewhere. Good afternoon, ladies." And he walked on.

He hadn't even looked at her, apart from that one brushing glance as he'd bowed. She should have been grateful. It made the encounter bearable.

So why did her heart ache and ache?

SEVERAL DAYS LATER, just over a week after the capture of the French spies and the retrieval of his paintings, he saw her again.

As he strode down the high street, she sat in the ice parlor with her sisters, Miss Grey, and Catherine Winslow. In spite of everything, his heart gave a huge leap. He missed her and the warmth of her family which somehow seemed part of her. And it was such a bright, laughing group he couldn't help but pause, his eyes devouring her face.

The last time he'd seen her, outside the Pump Room, he'd barely looked at her, aware it was bad luck the girls had seen him. Her whole manner had been repelling and cold, which was just what he'd wanted. And yet the awkwardness, the freezing civility between them had seemed somehow tragic after what had passed between them before. Seeing her again, even in that one glance, had churned him up. But he hadn't wavered. He knew he was doing the right thing. And, clearly, so did she.

But in secret, a man could look, just to remember and to assure himself she was well.

She was smiling at Miss Winslow, talking with, surely, just a little less animation than he remembered. She seemed pale to him, brittle, as though she might break. And her eyes...surely there was something *dull* about them? It didn't make her less beautiful, but it did make her look unspeakably sad.

Christ, did I do that to her?

And then the moment passed. She laughed at something Helen said, and he walked on hastily before she saw him.

But that look troubled him. He itched to paint it, but he longed, too, to wipe that sadness from her eyes and make her laugh with him as she'd done before. He walked faster in an effort to untwist his stomach, to diffuse the pain.

When he next paid attention to his surroundings, he found himself at the church and frowned in confusion. Surely he'd been heading homeward?

On impulse, he walked through the gate and up the path to the church. Since it seemed to be quiet within, he opened the door.

From the front pew, Tristram Grant turned his head and blinked. "Tamar?"

"In the flesh," Tamar replied flippantly, strolling up the aisle. "And at risk of being struck down."

Grant rose to meet him "Trust me, there have been wickeder men than you in here over the years, and none of them were struck down."

Tamar glanced at the books and papers the vicar had dropped on the front pew. "Don't you work at home?"

"Sometimes. Sometimes I get inspiration here, especially if Kate is out. She and Lady Serena are on a mission to make Catherine Winslow happy after Valère turned out to be what he was. Apparently, he had raised hopes."

There wasn't much Tamar could say to that. He was pretty sure he'd raised some of his own with as little right. Her last look at the hotel haunted him. And her pallor today.

"What can I do for you?" Grant asked.

"Oh, nothing," Tamar said awkwardly. "I was just passing. How is Lampton?"

"In pieces, though he'll never show it."

"Poor bastard," Tamar said, then glanced at the cross above the altar. "Sorry."

"It's a lesson to us all," Grant said, and it took Tamar a moment to realize he wasn't referring to bad language in church. "We have to seize the happiness of the day, and savor it, because we don't know when it might be taken from us."

Tamar searched his face. "If you mean Lady Serena, say so."

"I mean Lady Serena."

"Then you shouldn't. You know what I am, what I have—and don't have."

"Kate married me though I'm poor."

"You might be poor, but you have a respectable profession and prospects of promotion," Tamar retorted. "An ancient title is all that keeps me out of debtors' prison. And worse."

Grant frowned and sat down again. "What is this *worse* business? Did you mean what you said to her about murder?"

Tamar tugged one hand through his hair. "Of course, I meant it. It's true."

"Who did you kill?" Grant asked steadily.

Tamar's lips twisted. "A bailiff," he said, seating himself on the steps up the altar.

"Why?"

"Does it matter?"

"Oh, I think so."

Tamar shrugged. "Perhaps, but that isn't my story to tell."

"Then why did you tell her anything at all?"

Tamar rubbed absently at his healing shoulder, which had begun to ache again. "Because I wanted her to know the worst of me."

"To drive her away?"

"To make her understand," Tamar got out. "Why I cannot have her."

"She doesn't see that. She just saw you driving her away."

"Stop saying that."

"Then tell me the worst of you and let me judge from knowledge."

"I can't." Restlessly, Tamar began to rise again, but Grant grasped him by the good shoulder, pushing him back down.

"Tamar. You have to tell someone. It's eating you up."

"It isn't," Tamar denied. "Of course, it isn't,"

"Whatever you say. How old were you when you did it?"

Tamar shrugged. "Sixteen. I think. It doesn't really matter. Certainly, it was in the early years after my father died, and we had to leave school. We were all pretty much running wild about Tamar Abbey, while the house decayed around us. The servants had all left, or I'd sent them away because we couldn't pay them. But it was fun in an odd way, because I was too young or too stupid to think of the future. I thought I was looking after them if I scavenged some food for them. Hunting was fun and we cooked it together..."

He rubbed his forehead, trying to dismiss the memories. "And then we grew up. The day that Peter Rivers the bailiff came. They couldn't touch me for my father's debts, but they'd started to dun us about my late uncle's, claiming some of the few valuables still left in the house belonged to him. I sent them all away, but then Rivers came when I wasn't there. He tried to make my sisters hand over a Greek vase—I had a buyer lined up for that vase which would have fed us and clothed us all year. The girls refused, of course, but he was a bully. He really thought he could get away with it. They might have been a marquis's daughters, but they were poor and without protection and he no doubt thought he could make them too afraid to speak..."

He dropped his head into his hands. He didn't want to remember this. He didn't ever want to think of this. He swallowed. "He told them he would take payment in kind. You know what he meant. They didn't. They were fourteen years old. I can't talk about this."

"Jesus Christ," Grant whispered.

"When I got home, and rushed into the room, he had Anna by the throat, her dress ripped to shreds, and Christianne had just broken the Greek vase over his head. He was slightly dazed and still laughing when I flew at him. He had a dagger in his free hand—a Tamar dagger with our crest on it. I killed him with that as we fought..."

He raised his eyes to Grant's. "His brother saw us from the window. He saw the dagger go in. I swear to God I would have killed him, too, and buried him in the same unmarked grave as his brother, except that he ran."

There was silence in the church. Tamar wrapped it around himself like armor. He was sure somehow that he'd need it, as if the world would end now that he'd finally spoken these words.

Grant said, "If I were God, I would forgive you. I doubt I would forgive the man you killed."

Tamar's lips curved without permission. "But you're not God. You're my friend."

"Yes, I am."

"And you'll agree it's not the kind of story Serena should hear."

Grant's brow twitched. "She's a woman, Tamar, made of flesh and blood and understanding. Not a piece of precious porcelain. She won't break."

"She looks as if she might," Tamar blurted. "I saw her through the window of the ice parlor. I don't know if I'm a coxcomb or merely delusional to wonder if I did that to her."

"Yes, I think you did," Grant said brutally. "But cheer up. No one truly dies of a broken heart."

Tamar groaned. He felt as if he would. "Stop it, Grant. Apart from the insurmountable poverty, you don't know the end of Rivers' story. He waited two days, until I was calm, until I realized the magnitude of what I'd done. I couldn't give myself up. There was no one but Julian to take my place, to look after my family and what was left of my people. John Rivers knew that. And he watched me bury the body—or said he did."

"And he's been extorting payment for his silence ever since," Grant said quietly.

Tamar dragged a tired hand over his face. "I felt I still had to look after them. But our innocence was over. The boys ran wilder, went their own ways. In time, Anna grew a shell hard enough to break teeth on. At least Christianne retained her sweetness and married a good man. She and Anna will always look out for each other. Julian and Sylvester are grown up and making trouble of their own. So, I won't pay Rivers again. I'll stand trial."

"It won't come to that," Grant said. "It's past, Tamar. If you love Serena—and I think you truly do—offer her the man you are now, with all that you have now."

"A crumbling ruin and a debt the size of a Scottish island?"

Grant shrugged. "I could tell you you're a good man, a kind man with a rare artistic talent, and an even rarer gift of making people happy. The wealth difference is immaterial. Do you know she told Kate that Braithwaite's disapproval wouldn't matter? That she would simply wait until she was twenty-one and no longer needed his consent?"

Tamar dropped his hands, raising his gaze to Grant. "She said that?"

"Don't imagine you're doing her a favor, immolating yourself. You owe her happiness, not wealth."

"I've always believed they go together."

"No, you haven't. You're one of the happiest people I know, despite all the dross that's been flung at you over the years. None of it has broken you or your love of life. And you've never had a penny."

Tamar regarded him, trying in vain to prevent the hope leaping in his emotion-battered heart. "I think you see the world very differently from most people."

"No. I just help some people see it from a different perspective."

"I don't think most people would agree with the perspective that I would be granting Serena Conway a favor by offering her marriage!"

"Well," Grant said, leaning back and gathering his papers. "You have to decide if they're right. Or if you are."

Tamar threw his head back, lying right down on the steps. "I hurt her, I know I did, I thought it was for the best. I was trying to be good. And I don't know if she'll forgive me."

"She probably won't," Grant said flatly and grinned at Tamar's appalled look. "At first. You'll need all your charm. And a little time."

Chapter Fourteen

K ATE GRANT KEPT a box at the theatre. "It's the one extravagance I've maintained," she told Serena. "Well, apart from the carriage. And the horses."

The theatre party consisted of Kate and Serena, escorted by Bernard Muir, Mr. and Miss Winslow, and the Penhalligan—they of the following week's rout. So, it was a lively party, and Serena, who loved the theatre, was determined to enjoy it, to pull herself out of this slough of longing.

Until she recognized the first actress on stage. The woman who had kissed Tamar at the hotel that night. Then, of course, she had to pretend not to notice, or at least not to be upset. So, keeping the faint smile plastered on her face, she let her gaze stray from the stage. Most people spent more time watching the audience than the play in any case.

It was a small theatre compared with those she'd attended in London, and it was easy to recognize old friends and acquaintances in the boxes opposite. They smiled and bowed to her, and she nodded back and continued her perusal down to the pit where, inevitably, a few young bucks lurked among the lower orders, ogling the ladies as well as the actresses.

Almost casually, her gaze met Lord Tamar's. It didn't surprise her, not really, but still the world tilted. What did surprise her was that this time, he didn't look away. Instead, his lips gave the funny upward quirk that had so intrigued her on first acquaintance, and he inclined his head.

In case anyone was watching, she gave the briefest of nods in return and transferred her attention back to the stage—where his actress, thankfully, no longer held forth.

It didn't matter that he hadn't come for her, that it changed nothing. His very presence was enough to sweep away the lingering dullness of the evening, churning her stomach once more into all the old turmoil of anticipation, anxiety, and yearning. She couldn't change that. She just had to acknowledge that it meant nothing. It never had.

And yet the walls of her certainty had already crumbled slightly. Mr. Grant had explained something of Tamar's harrowing story. She could not but feel pity for his terrified sisters, and for the boy consumed by guilt because he felt he'd failed to defend them, and yet had taken a life. Which he'd been paying for ever since. Literally. Part of her yearned to hold him and soothe away his pain. Part of her admired that none of his losses, none of his difficulties faced so young, had broken him.

It explained a little about his rejection of her. And yet, the fact that Grant was the one who had had to tell her added to the hurt. In the end, it changed nothing.

At the first interval, the true purpose of the theatre for most people began—calling on friends and acquaintances in other boxes. And Kate's box was one of the busiest. For once, Serena had no idea what had gone on in the farce. All her focus was on proving to Tamar that she wasn't remotely interested in his presence, let alone bothered by it. So, after allowing the Penhalligan boy and an almost unknown man to compete for her attention for a full ten minutes, she allowed herself a surreptitious glance into the pit.

He wasn't there.

Of course, he wasn't. He was in the dressing room of that woman. Or just visiting wealthier friends in their boxes. She was so sure he would not approach Kate's, that his arrival deprived her of breath.

He wore his own usual clothes, Braithwaite's having been returned laundered and brushed earlier in the week, and looked as carelessly handsome and tousled as ever. He seemed to make his way through the throng directly toward her, causing her pulse to leap with mingled outrage and pleasure. But of course, he was approaching Kate, not Serena. And once he'd civilly greeted Kate, he sat next to Catherine for a few moments.

I don't care. I don't care. Damn him, how dare he come in here...?

"Lady Serena." Despite all her plans for aloofness, his voice made her jump. She leaned back behind the curtain to hide her suddenly hot cheeks, and as Catherine rose in response to Kate's beckoning, he sat in the vacant chair, drawing it closer to hers. Now they were almost cut off from everyone else.

"I came to apologize," he said, low.

"Apology accepted." That at least was cold and aloof.

"You haven't heard what I'm apologizing for yet," he pointed out.

"I know what you *should* apologize for."

"I shouldn't have spoken to you as I did in the hotel. It was unforgivable, but I hope you can forgive me in time."

"It is nothing," she said remotely. "Already forgotten."

He blinked. "You've forgotten that I accused myself of murder?"

"Oh hush, of course I haven't forgotten *that*," she said crossly, glancing beyond him to see if anyone could have overheard. Almost reluctantly, her gaze came back to his. "*That* is what you are apologizing for?" she asked, to be sure.

He shrugged. "For my whole manner to you at that encounter. It was rude and hurtful, and my only excuse is my own pain in feeling it necessary to renounce you, to give you up before I'd even won you."

Oh, I was won. That's what is unforgivable. She bit down on her lip to keep the words in. "Then you're not apologizing for the lies you told me during the rest of our acquaintance?" she managed at last.

"Oh no. There were no lies. I meant every word I said to you. And I've come to see that I wasn't wrong. Your happiness, not your family's or my supposed honor, should always have been my concern. If I can make you happy, I'll want no more of life."

He was doing it again. She couldn't believe he was doing it again, luring her in and she was so desperate to fall for it.

"Well, you can't," she said flatly.

"Then you won't marry me?"

She stared at him. There was understanding in his eyes as well as a rueful pleading that almost won her over. "No," she said with as much hauteur as she could manage. She thought it pretty well done.

But he only smiled. "I thought you'd say that, so I want to assure you I won't give up. And I will win you."

"Oh, no. I only allow one chance and you lost yours. You most certainly can't win me now."

He leaned forward, as if he were looking beyond the curtain into the main part of the theatre, but it brought his head close to hers, almost touching. His breath kissed her ear. "I wasn't really trying to win you before. I was just following instinct and desire and fun. Now, I'm serious."

She jerked her head around, which most certainly brought her too close to his lips. She remembered their devastating effect on her. The idea of him being more intense, more determined, melted her very bones.

"What nonsense you talk," she said distinctly. "Go away, Lord Tamar."

"For now," he breathed, rising to his feet.

And only with his threatened departure did she remember what Grant had told her, why he'd committed that murder he was suffering for still.

"My lord,"

He sat back down, expectantly.

"How are your sisters?" she managed.

His eyes were almost frightened as they searched hers, and then, slowly, they softened. "They are well," he said. "Thank you."

She wasn't softening, truly she wasn't, but she was glad she'd said it.

And if her heart drummed at the prospect of his courtship, his pursuit, well, that was most definitely her secret.

HE DIDN'T COME all the next day.

She knew he wouldn't. She couldn't receive gentlemen visitors, not formally, at any rate, and he would only have been turned away at the door. It didn't stop her watching the approach from the drive, or walking twice in the orchard. She laughed at herself, but in truth, she wanted him to be there so she could soothe her own humiliation by rejecting him. In fact, she wished he would make a formal offer for her hand so that she could laugh in his face.

Her stomach dived.

Is that really what she would do? Laugh?

Or make a dignified exit from the room?

She wouldn't get the chance to do either. Braithwaite would throw him out before the offer even got to her.

She just couldn't fathom Tamar's purpose in this.

THE FOLLOWING DAY, Mrs. Winslow and Catherine made a detour in their journey into Blackhaven, and took Serena up in their carriage. Kate was "at home" that afternoon.

"It's very kind of you," Serena said, gratefully, as she joined them in the carriage. "But I have to warn you that you are aiding and abetting me in breaking my mother's rules. You must know I am in disgrace and not meant to go out."

"My dear, I know you *go* out," Mrs. Winslow returned, "and I believe the countess would rather you do so properly chaperoned. Besides, I'm sure she does not wish the world to know she regards you as disgraced. Mrs. Grant thinks she will already have reached that conclusion herself."

"Let us hope so," Serena murmured.

The first person she saw when she entered Kate's drawing room was Lord Tamar. The immediate hammering of her heart was, she assured herself, a response to the challenge of remaining aloof.

And it was a challenge. As soon as she'd been welcomed by her hosts, he was there beside her, offering her his chair, and when she took it, he perched casually on the arm beside her. In anyone else, it would have looked proprietorial, if not scandalous. But Tamar made his own rules, and Blackhaven society seemed to regard his social oddities with indulgence.

It was Serena who found it difficult to concentrate on the general conversation, to do more than smile and nod when something seemed to be expected of her. For her whole being was aware of Tamar's closeness, of every smallest movement of his large, lean body.

At last, he murmured, "How are you?"

"I am well, thank you," she returned civilly. "How is your wound?"

He flexed his injured shoulder. "Pretty much healed. Would you like to ride with me, tomorrow? Grant is lending me one of his horses."

It took her breath away. "I thank you, but I cannot tomorrow," she managed.

"Why not? Are you afraid?"

She glared up at him. "Of what should I possibly be afraid?"

"Nothing," he replied at once. "So why won't you come?"

"Because I do not wish to," she snapped.

"Then you won't meet me in the orchard either?"

"You are quite correct. I won't."

"Please, Serena," he breathed. "I won't give up."

"Then you will waste your life," she said flippantly and rose to her feet. Inevitably, he stood with her, bringing her for an instant so close that they almost touched. Their eyes met. Her bones melted and her heart twisted with a yearning she refused to give into. "Excuse me," she muttered and walked away to join Catherine.

SHE DIDN'T GO to the orchard the following morning, though she lay awake for some time, staring at the window and refusing to regret it.

Later on, after breakfast, she returned to her chamber, trying to decide which gown would look best for the Penhalligans' rout tomorrow evening. For some reason, such things mattered again.

Then, something in the mirror caught her attention. In the window's reflection, a man was crossing the lawn beyond the courtyard.

Dropping her favored gown on the floor in her hurry, she sped to the window. She knew, long before he was close enough to make out his features, that it was Tamar. His loping stride and long, lean figure, the shape of all the paraphernalia he always carried, made it clear.

Breathlessly, she returned to the glass to make sure her hair was properly pinned and her face not streaked with flour, for she'd been helping Cook bake for the harvest party on Saturday. Then she rushed downstairs to the small drawing room, and assumed a languid pose on the sofa with her book. It could have been upside down for all the true attention she paid it.

Before long, she heard the knock, heard his voice in the hall below, greeting Paton and joking with the footman. They didn't deny him entry, for she heard footsteps on the stairs and thought her heart would burst with excitement or at least with the challenge of appearing indifferent as she asked him to leave. For some reason, it was very important to appear indifferent.

But she waited in vain. The footsteps faded. No one came near the small drawing room.

She rang the bell. When the footman appeared she said, "Did I not hear a visitor, James?"

"Lord Tamar, my lady. He's painting the young ladies in the schoolroom. He said not to disturb you."

"Not to dist—" She broke off, furious with him.

She was already storming down the passages to the schoolroom before it struck her that this was no doubt what he wanted her to do. If he'd called and politely requested to paint, she would either have refused and dismissed him, or agreed and not gone near the schoolroom. This way ensured she stormed in there, flustered and wrong-footed because she'd already given her permission for him to paint her sisters, before all this trouble.

She paused, took a deep breath, and walked much more slowly, modelling herself on Kate at her most languid.

Rather to her surprise, no chattering or laughter spilled through the open schoolroom door, and when she paused in the doorway, the girls all had their heads down, working. Miss Grey, an expression of awe on her face, watched from her own desk. A few feet away, Lord Tamar had set up his easel and was busily painting. As he glanced up and met Serena's gaze, a spontaneous smile curved his lips, and her heart turned over.

But she couldn't give in to this, not again. She walked into the room, directly toward Miss Grey.

"Serena!" Alice exclaimed, just a little nervously, for they all knew there was some quarrel between Serena and Tamar. "Lord Tamar came to paint us after all."

"In your unnatural state of quiet study?" Serena said.

"He says we're not allowed to move," Helen threw in.

"You don't obey when *I* tell you that," Serena said.

The girls laughed.

"Go and have a peek, Serena," Maria urged. "Tell us what it looks like so far."

"Absolutely not," Serena said.

By then, Miss Grey had stood up to greet her.

Tamar, who hadn't given more than a nod and a smile over the top of his easel, said now, "I hope you don't mind. I came to keep my promise to your sisters."

Then where is Kate Grant? Her mouth opened to say the words just as she caught sight of Kate sitting in the corner with her book. She looked up and waved. Where the devil had she come from? She must have been here already, waiting for him.

Serena closed her mouth. *Traitress.* "Why should I mind?" she said carelessly. "So long as you don't interrupt their lessons—Miss Grey has the final word."

"Actually, his presence is less disruptive than yours," Miss Grey said. "My lady."

Tamar laughed. So did the girls, and Serena was sure Kate sniggered behind her book. They were all in league against her, or at least *for* Tamar. How could so many sensible, kind people be urging this madness?

Because it's what I want. Because he makes me happy.

Made *me happy. I can't trust him anymore.*

Couldn't she? Couldn't she understand his doubts, his misplaced honor? A lump rose in her throat.

"Then carry on, of course," she managed.

Almost blindly, she turned and left the room. She needed to be alone in her own chamber, to cry, to throw things, to think…

"Serena."

She didn't stop for his voice behind her. She couldn't. Instinctively, she quickened her pace, but inevitably, he caught up with her, grasping her elbow to make her halt. The passage was empty and silent. Presumably peace reigned once more in the schoolroom.

"I'm sorry," he said softly. "I don't want to hurt you."

"Then why do you keep coming back?"

He stared at her, then placed both hands on her shoulders. "Because I love you. Because I think I might have made a mistake in believing you'd be happier without me."

She lifted her chin, hanging on to her pride by a thread. "Whatever gave you that idea?"

"Grant, mainly. And Kate. They made me think, *truly* think, and now I'm trusting my heart over my brain." His fingers tightened on her shoulders. "Couldn't you be happy with me, Serena? Don't you love me?"

She closed her eyes, as if that could hide her from him. "I would have given anything for you, stood up to anyone and anything. But you *spoiled* it, Tamar."

There was a pause, then, but she didn't open her eyes. Instead, she tried to turn her head away, but his fingers caught her chin, tilting up her face.

"No, I didn't," he whispered. "I just gave it a bit of a setback. Nothing is perfect, Serena, least of all me. But the love was always there, growing stronger with every instant. That is all I have."

His mouth closed on hers, tender and sweet. She allowed it for an instant, because it felt so good, so curiously right. But then a tear escaped the corner of her eye and she gasped, freeing herself, and fled along the passage to the stairs.

WHEN TAMAR LEFT his studio to attend Mrs. Penhalligan's rout, Rivers was back on his step.

"Still here?" Tamar said, locking his door. "You really don't know what else to do, do you? Go home, Rivers, you'll get nothing from me."

"Then, it'll go badly for you," Rivers called after him. "I'm warning you."

Tamar laughed and went on his way, eager to get to the party, to see Serena again. He knew she would be there, and after their unexpectedly emotional encounter outside the castle schoolroom, he had hopes that he was winning. He was sure she cared for him still. She was just afraid to give in. He wasn't proud that he'd caused that fear.

Mrs. Penhalligan looked both gratified and slightly dazed by the sheer quantity and quality of the guests packed into her modest house. Of course, once Serena and Kate had decided to "help", the poor lady hadn't stood a chance. At least the success of her party was assured.

Tamar found it rather touching that they would go to such lengths to cheer Catherine after her disastrous flirtation with Valère. As well as distracting her, they were restoring her confidence, showing her how popular and attractive she was. It wasn't difficult with so many of her old Blackhaven friends present, which in turn brought curious strangers to be introduced.

It could have gone horribly wrong, of course, for both Kate and Serena were more stunningly beautiful and eye-catching than the much quieter Catherine. Kate might have been the vicar's wife and out of bounds, but Serena was not.

Discovered in the main drawing room, vivacious and dazzling in a gown of white muslin over rose silk, she set his blood on fire. She was leading the applause for one of the Penhalligan girls who had just performed on the harp, at the same time as she casually led two very obvious admirers to mix in Catherine's court. Not that she was so obvious as to palm every gentleman off on Catherine. Some, she introduced to one or other of the Penhalligan girls, forming larger groups from which she then flitted off to join another set. She was like a butterfly, lovely and never still.

"Well?" Kate said, joining him by the drawing room wall, where he leaned, watching Serena.

"I was just thinking," Tamar mused, "what a wonderful partner and asset she would be for a clever man with political or other ambitions."

"She would be," Kate agreed. "So would I. In a different style, of course."

He glanced at her. "And yet you chose Grant. At least he is a good man."

"He says you are. Getting cold feet, Tamar?"

"No," he said in genuine surprise. "I was thinking how anything would be possible for even a wicked man, if she were at his side."

It was true. As he made his way across the room, greeting acquaintances and pausing for a word with the young people of the house, the world seemed to be expanding. He'd never thought further ahead than earning a few coins for his pictures, to put food in his and his siblings' mouths, and get Rivers off his back for another year. But although he loved to paint, and knew he always would, he knew, too, that a lot of what he produced was pretty dross, souvenirs for visitors or flattering portraits for the wealthy. There were better things he could do, to make a difference.

"I thought you had come to speak to me," Serena said tartly. "But apparently not."

Only then did he realize he'd stopped in front of her, his mind rushing with ideas and possibilities while his mouth remained mute.

He grinned. "I have. Your beauty leaves me tongue-tied."

"If only."

"Walk with me?" he invited.

She glanced uncertainly to her left.

"There is no room for me at Catherine's court," he said wryly. "It's you I want to talk to."

"What about?" she asked discouragingly, although she did walk beside him.

"To ask your advice. Do you think it would help or hinder my cause if I sent Braithwaite the painting of your sisters, along with a letter asking for your hand?"

Her face flushed. "I don't think it would make any difference. He will refuse and probably post up here—with my mother!—before either of us can draw breath."

"Then at least I'll be able to speak to him."

She looked at him. "It isn't his consent you need."

"Most."

A frown tugged her brow. "I beg your pardon?"

"It isn't his consent I need *most*," he said patiently. "I understand that. But I'm planning ahead."

She looked as if she didn't know whether to laugh or deliver a blistering retort. Taking advantage of her indecision, he smiled. "Shall we see if there's any supper?"

"I suppose you haven't eaten today."

"I suppose I haven't. Julian's winnings are all gone, and I'm still waiting for Alban to cough up."

"You like being outrageous, don't you?"

"Just honest. Ah, look, here is the dining room, and no one has discovered it yet. Meet me in the orchard tomorrow."

He liked taking her by surprise. Though in this case, he was really just trying to say what he had to before anyone else joined them, as happened almost immediately. Seeing him and Serena peep in, several other people spilled out from the card room as well as the drawing room to partake of the elegant supper.

"Well?" Tamar breathed.

"Quite well, thank you," Serena replied distantly. "This tart is delicious. Good evening, Mr. Halford, how are you?"

Tamar let it be.

Chapter Fifteen

Before she went to sleep on the night of the Penhalligan's rout, Serena told herself she would not go to the orchard in the morning. Or if she did, she'd wait for at least half an hour after seeing him go in. She half-hoped she'd wake up too late.

But in fact, she woke up early, her heart already beating with excitement because she knew she *would* go. Just to see what he would say, of course.

She went early, while the girls were still eating breakfast. She wrapped a hooded cloak over her favorite old gown, for it was not a bright, autumnal day like the first time she'd met him. Instead, there was a fine drizzle misting down from grey skies. It should have felt ominous, yet she liked the cool wetness on her upturned face. The mist seemed to envelop her in in a bubble of secret elation.

He wouldn't come, obviously. They were playing a game…

"I thought you'd make me wait." His voice spoke behind her, warming her.

She smiled into the rain without turning. "I thought about it. But it seems I don't care for games any more. So, I thought I'd talk to you instead."

"I'm glad."

He was closer now, so close she wasn't surprised when his hands touched her wrists, and glided up her cloaked arms. She half-turned her head, looking up into his face. His eyes were serious and warm with feeling, but close behind the calmness he strived for, she sensed a profound turbulence that moved her. Perhaps it was his quickened breathing that gave him away.

"Do you forgive me?" he asked hoarsely.

"Oh, for what?" she said, her voice catching. "For doing what everyone would tell you was the honorable thing? You should have talked to me, told me..."

"I couldn't find the words. I still can't. Just know that I love you, that I would die to give you one instant of happiness..."

She rose on tiptoe, reaching up for his mouth. He gave it, fervently. She fell back against him and his arms closed around her. The rain pattered down on her face, and his, seeping into their mouths as they kissed and kissed again.

She turned in his arms, throwing hers around his neck, and pressing her cheek to his. "Does this mean you will marry me?" she asked huskily.

She felt his smile in her hair. "It means I insist upon it," he murmured. "Only how do I convince your brother I'm not a fortune hunter?"

"I don't really see that you can," she said ruefully. "He doesn't know you. And by the time he does, if he ever does, I imagine I will already be twenty-one and we can be married anyway. Or we could elope to Scotland."

"Like Dax," he said thoughtfully. He frowned. "You would really do that to be with me?"

"Of course, I would." She was rewarded with a kiss that curled her toes. Before it ended, his arms were around her beneath the cloak and his hard body pressed intimately to hers.

He groaned. "It will all but kill me to wait, but I can't do that to you. The scandal of an elopement would be horrendous and I won't drive a wedge between you and your family if I can avoid it."

"We may not avoid it. It depends how stupid Braithwaite decides to be over the issue," Serena said with sisterly candor.

"Well, we might as well begin as soon as possible. I'll write to him today."

"So will I," Serena said, kissing his lips just because they were so close and she liked it so much.

After the last couple of weeks, she couldn't believe how happy she was. She couldn't contain it, but began to sway in his arms, and a moment later, was being danced through the trees, waltzing in the rain and laughing with sheer exuberance.

"Oh, stop, stop," she gasped at last, still laughing. "Someone will see us! Or hear. Or worse, I'll collapse on the mud."

"I won't let you," he assured her, but he did stop, leaning his back against the wet trunk of the big apple tree and taking her face between his hands. His eyes seemed to blaze, thrilling her all over again. "Do you know what I would like most?"

She shook her head, smiling with anticipation.

"I'd like to make love to you under this tree, in the moonlight."

Desire flamed through her. "Instead of on the cellar floor?" she managed, recalling a previous improper suggestion.

"Both," he growled, and kissed her hard, with wicked sensuality. And when she couldn't suppress a little moan of pleasure and need, he gentled the kiss, and smiled against her lips. "For now, I'll settle for dancing with you. Is there to be dancing at this satanic beach revel of yours?"

She gave a gurgle of laughter. "It is not remotely satanic! The Winslows and all the strict old biddies from town have agreed to come. But yes, we have hired an orchestra! They were not keen at first for fear of getting sand in their instruments, but we have promised them a canopy and, I suspect, an enormous amount of money. And they have agreed to come."

"Then I want two waltzes. With or without rain." He freed her reluctantly, placing her hand in his arm to walk more decorously toward the path.

"I wish you could simply come in and have breakfast with us," she blurted. "The girls always like to see you."

"One day," he said lightly. "One day soon, we may see each other whenever we like." For an instant, his eyes blazed again. "And make love whenever we like."

"YOU HAVE MADE it up with Tamar," Kate said, as soon as Serena danced across the drawing room to greet her.

Serena laughed. "Is it so obvious?"

"Blindingly." Kate smiled and gave her a quick hug. "I am so glad for you! But you do realize the real fight is yet to come?"

Serena wrinkled her nose. "I know. I am prepared for it. Tamar has written to Braithwaite. So have I. In a few days, I daresay I shall receive a stinker of a letter summoning me to London, or heralding his furious arrival with my mother in toe. To be honest, I am so prepared for their refusal that I shan't let it cast me down. It is barely three months until my birthday, after all."

"They may refuse to receive him altogether," Kate warned.

"I know."

To please them, she was already observing strict propriety within the castle. Tamar never called, except with Kate to paint the children. Outside the house, they met in the orchard every morning—which might prove more difficult with her lady mother and Braithwaite in residence, but she would find a way. Being alone with him was a time she valued too much to give up, not just because it allowed her a taste of passion, but because they could talk freely and much more intimately than in public.

Without going into distressing details, he'd told her something of the attack that had led to his killing of the bailiff, and more about its effect on himself and his siblings. Beneath his good-natured exterior, he carried a huge weight of guilt over everything concerned with it, and that, she thought, was the reason he'd paid Rivers all those years. It was a vain attempt to pay for his guilt, to assuage it. Because he thought he should.

"If he'd been charged with what he did, he would have hanged," Serena had told him. "You spared him that, and your sisters the inevitable scandal. I don't honestly see what you could have done differently, or even better. And you were really only a child yourself."

He'd touched her cheek with tenderness, a rueful smile playing on his lips. "You are biased. And very sweet." And yet, as he'd kissed her, she thought she might have lightened his burden just a little, not so much by her words as by her acceptance of his past.

"Well," she said brightly now to Kate, "I think all is prepared for the revel tonight! Tamar and Jem have rigged up some very ingenious pulleys to convey things like food and drink down to the cove without the servants having to trek up and down the path all the time."

In the end, they had decided to hold the event at Braithwaite Cove rather than the town beach. It provided a little more privacy and a sense of respectable intimacy, without being exactly on Braithwaite property. Inevitably, Brathwaite servants were involved, of course, but so were Kate's, the Winslows' and a few others. And Serena was not the hostess. Kate and Mrs. Winslow shared that honor.

Still, Serena was aware she was further breaking both the spirit and the letter of her confinement in the castle. It would, inevitably, be added to her list of crimes when her mother discovered it. With luck, it would be a distant memory by the time the subject came up and she was obliged to confess.

For now, she prepared to enjoy the event to the full, particularly her promised waltzes with Tamar. She accompanied Kate to the schoolroom, where Tamar was continuing his painting of the girls. Although she'd already seen him that morning in the orchard, her heart quickened at the sight of him already behind his easel and mixing paint on his palette. His spontaneous smile of greeting melted her all over again.

"You are quite ridiculously in love," Kate murmured in her ear, though oddly, she sounded neither disapproving nor scoffing. Serena guessed she was "ridiculously" in love with her own husband and recognized the signs in others.

"So, *may* we come to the revel?" Maria demanded as soon as she saw Serena.

Serena, having already discussed the matter with Miss Grey and Mrs. Winslow, finally relented. "Well, you may, but only for an hour.

Catherine's younger brother and sister will be there for that time, too. But you must stay with Miss Grey and be on your best behavior at all times."

"Oh, we will," Alice said fervently.

Serena went over to examine the painting, which had really caught the character of her sisters, the hint of mischief, resignation, and concentration in their eyes. "Hmm...am I mad to let them loose at such an event?"

BRAITHWAITE COVE WAS a blaze of light, burning torches attached to the cliff side and myriad lanterns aiding the natural glow of the full moon. A couple of braziers surrounded by chairs had been placed close to the cliff for the comfort of the frailer guests. Against the fickle weather, two canopies had been set up, the largest for the guests, the smaller for the musical quartet. But it seemed the weather would behave itself for once. The sky was clear and starry, bringing cold but no spirit-dampening rain.

The guests moved about constantly, liveried servants passing between them to offer champagne or tea or something stronger for the gentlemen. Although no one wore their best ball gowns for the occasion, the flashes of color beneath fur-lined cloaks and the wink of jewels in the ladies' hair all helped to create a wonderful picture.

Or so Tamar thought as he strolled along the beach with a few friends. Inevitably, his gaze was drawn at once by Serena, not just because he loved her, but because she flitted among the guests like the butterfly he'd once thought her, distributing fun and laughter.

"She has to be the most beautiful girl ever," Fenner, one of Tamar's friends, said reverently.

"Yes, well, she's the Earl of Braithwaite's sister," Lieutenant Gordon retorted, "so she's a cut above you, old chap!"

"A man can look."

Tamar could hardly blame him for looking. He couldn't take his eyes off her himself. The musicians struck up, and she began to dance with Bernard Muir in a country dance set that kicked up sand and caused much innocent hilarity. Among the other dancers, Tamar recognized Catherine Winslow, the younger Braithwaite ladies, and a gaggle of Penhalligans. Among the youngest dancers at least, the sex of one's partner did not appear to matter.

"Well, Muir's dancing with her," Fenner pointed out. "She ain't high in the instep. I shall ask for a waltz."

"I'll wager you five pounds," Tamar said. "that her waltzes are spoken for."

"Done," Fenner said promptly.

"Idiot," said Gordon. "Tamar only bets when he knows he'll win."

Tamar smiled serenely.

"Evening, gents," said a voice close by, and a man sitting on a rock tipped his hat to them. Rivers.

Tamar scowled. He'd wondered why the bailiff hadn't been haunting his doorstep the last couple of days. He'd obviously taken Tamar's last words to heart and decided to change his tactics to haunt him in public instead. Not that it would make any difference. Tamar still wouldn't pay him. But he didn't want the little rat spoiling Serena's evening. Or Catherine's, since this had been created primarily for her, and the squire's daughter was a sweet girl.

"Who the devil is that?" Gordon demanded. "Damned sure he ain't invited. Shall I move him on?"

"You can try," Tamar returned. "But it's a public beach. Unless he annoys anyone, I'd ignore him."

They walked on to greet Mrs. Winslow and then Kate, who were welcoming guests from either approach to the beach.

In recognition of the uneven and unconventional dance floor, each dance was considerably shorter than usual. The orchestra allowed recovery time, playing some gentle chamber music between dances.

Tamar, being circumspect in the vain hope of not appalling Braithwaite more than necessary, didn't immediately rush at Serena as soon as her dance ended. However, Fenner, determined to try his luck and, no doubt, to win his five pounds, had positioned himself strategically close by. Tamar and Gordon chose to join him there.

Serena's sisters at once greeted Tamar with their usual affection, and he made general introductions to his friends.

"You have escaped Miss Grey," he said to the girls.

"Only briefly," Helen assured him. "Will *you* dance with us, sir?"

"What, all of you at once? I think that might get confusing for everyone else. I'll do it one at a time, though, if Lady Serena permits?"

"Gladly," Serena said, clearly torn between amusement and gratitude.

"Lady Serena, might I beg the honor of a waltz with you?" Fenner blurted.

"Sadly, I am already promised for both."

It was part of her charm that she sounded genuinely regretful. Tamar, not so kind-hearted, merely grinned at his friend as the music halted and changed to a waltz. He offered his arm to Serena.

Fenner glowered at him. "Tamar, you—"

"Told you," Gordon interrupted. "Miss Winslow, dare I hope you are not promised already?"

"What was that about?" Serena asked as they waltzed together across the sand.

"I wagered Fenner he didn't stand a chance of waltzing with you."

"I'm not sure I care to have my name bandied about in wagers."

"Look on the bright side. I now have five pounds with which to buy you a betrothal gift."

"Don't do that," she said at once. "Buy something for yourself."

He allowed his arm to tighten just a little around her. "I already have all I want. Do you think anyone would notice if I held you beneath the cloak?"

"I'm fairly sure they would," she said, breathlessly enough to inflame him. "Besides, you just said you had all you wanted."

"I lied."

Serena laughed, attracting the attention of several dancers around her. She lowered her voice. "Do you think everyone knows about us?

Besides Kate and Mr. Grant."

He shrugged. "I really don't care."

SOMETIME LATER, AFTER he'd danced with each of the girls, then Catherine and Kate, he strolled among the revelers with a glass of what could only be contraband brandy. That was when he caught sight of Rivers again.

RIVERS WAS UP to something. Perhaps he actually planned to denounce Tamar in public. For himself, Tamar didn't care what people said or thought, but he couldn't allow it to touch Serena, or even to spoil her evening. Maybe Gordon had been right. Maybe it was time to send the bastard about his business. But as he watched, another figure came loping over the beach after Rivers, who turned and spoke to him. Both looked toward the revelers.

Distracted by Mr. Winslow, Tamar returned his attention to the party.

A little later, after dancing with a young lady whose name he couldn't remember and restoring her to her mother, Miss Grey asked him if he'd seen Helen.

"Lady Serena thinks they should return to the castle now," she said. "The Winslow children have already left."

"I'll bring her back to you," he promised, appreciating her difficulty in keeping hold of the first two girls while searching for the third.

He found Helen without much difficulty, dancing back and forth over some rocks at the edge of the cove. "Your presence is required, Lady Helen," he said with mock formality.

She wrinkled her nose, much as Serena did. "I suppose we have had rather more than an hour."

"I suppose you have," he agreed as they walked back together.

"Who is that man?" she asked, pointing across the cove to the figure he'd seen before, talking to Rivers. Now he stood on the edge of the party, scratching his head.

"I don't know," he said. Rivers was hovering farther back as though waiting for something. Again, unease twisted through him. "He isn't one of the guests."

"I know. But he asked about you."

Tamar frowned. "What? He spoke to you?"

"With perfect politeness," Helen said with what she must have imagined was reassurance. "He just asked which of the gentlemen was Lord Tamar."

"Did he, by God?" His disquiet sharpened. This man had been talking to Rivers. Had Rivers finally called in the law? A Bow Street runner, perhaps? He had to put this off until after the party, or at least leave now... "Did you point me out?" he asked Helen casually.

"Well, no. Fortunately, I couldn't see you at the time, and I wasn't sure it was his business in any case."

"What a very perceptive person you are... Now, you have to run straight to Miss Grey by the left-hand brazier, for this is the dance your sister promised me."

"I'll go," Helen agreed reluctantly, but he kept half an eye on her progress as he approached Serena.

"You again," Serena said happily as he swept her into the waltz.

"In the flesh." He loved the feel of her soft, lithe body moving in his arms. The sense of pleasure, frustration and anticipation was unique. He smiled. "I think you and Kate may congratulate yourselves on a most successful party."

"Do you know, I think we may," she said complacently. "I'm certainly enjoying it."

"So am I, though of course I enjoy anything that allows me to hold you. Serena, I think I'm going to leave now. There's a man looking for me—"

"Rivers," she said at once.

"Well, no, but—"

"Rivers," she repeated. "He's coming toward us."

Tamar spun her around so that he could see what she had, and sure enough, Rivers was actually approaching among the guests.

"I'll draw him away," Tamar said curtly, releasing her.

But she clung to his hand determinedly. "*We* shall draw him away," she corrected. "It would look most singular if you left me in the middle of the dance."

"Serena—"

"A gentle stroll, for I have danced too much," she insisted.

He gave in, for the moment, and as they walked a little way apart from the dancers, Rivers swerved and followed them. Tamar's plan was to avoid him until the waltz ended, then part from Serena, and hasten back along the beach, drawing Rivers and, hopefully Rivers' friend, with him. Somehow, he'd try and find a way to deal with the accusations quietly. He didn't want Serena touched by them, and he was damned sure Braithwaite wouldn't.

But Serena took him surprise, walking all over his plan at the out-set by tugging him toward the bailiff.

"Serena," he warned, low. "This is not the best way."

"On the contrary, it's the only way," she said with unexpected grimness. "It's time this ended."

"I couldn't agree more."

By then, Rivers had come to a halt directly in front of them and stood, smirking. "What now, *my lord*? Prepared to pay up? Or will I explain our business to the lady and all her friends?"

"We have no business," Tamar said coldly. "And you were not invited. Good evening."

"Invited or not, I'll say what needs to be said!" Rivers gloated.

"Go ahead," Serena invited. She even stood aside, gesturing with her hand toward the guests. Both Tamar and Rivers blinked at her, stunned.

"Go ahead," she repeated. "Make your silly allegations to Lord Tamar's friends. If they don't laugh at you, they'll call the Watch."

"It is I who have called the Watch!" Rivers blustered.

"For what purpose?" Serena asked. She sounded more amused than frightened. "You think to have Lord Tamar, a peer of the realm, clapped up and put on trial? By his peers? Who include my brother, by the by, soon to be Lord Tamar's brother-in-law. He has taken his seat and already has much influence, I believe."

This clearly, was news to Rivers, who blinked rapidly, as though trying to assimilate this unexpected information.

Serena's face betrayed nothing but contempt. "Do you seriously imagine that any jury of his peers would condemn Lord Tamar for what he did to such a vile creature who had assaulted his orphaned sisters in their own home? Fool, it's you who'd hang for conspiracy in such a crime, and for trying to profit from it. Begone, or my people will remove you."

And with that, she turned on her heel. Since her hand was still in his arm, Tamar swung around with her, his gaze fixed to her face in awe. Not just for how she'd defended him and dealt with Rivers, but for seeing quite suddenly what had always been in front of his face.

There *were* privileges to his title and birth, advantages beyond being able to escape debtors' prison, and even charges of murder. It was all a little vague yet, but he had a seat in the House of the Lords, in the parliament of the realm. There were ways for him to make a difference.

All this buzzed in the back of his mind as he gazed at Serena in total admiration.

She glanced up at him, and emitted a shaky laugh. "Well, it had to be said. And you are too eaten by guilt to see it."

"Then you believe it to be true?"

"Of course it is true. And Rivers knows it."

Tamar began to smile. "What a truly magnificent being you are. I wish I knew why you loved me."

"It must be your modesty. Or your flattery."

"Shall we return to our waltz?" he suggested, taking her into his arms just a little too early.

Only as he spun her around did he see Rivers's friend, almost right beside them. He looked like the roughest of sailors crammed into a respectable suit.

"Lord Tamar?" this individual said sternly.

"Oh God," Serena said at almost the same time, though her gaze was not on Rivers's friend but on the foot of the cliff path, where stood a formidable matron with a rigid back and a younger, handsome man with a face like thunder. The suspicion had only begun to form in Tamar's brain before Serena said tragically. "Oh no. It's my mother. And Braithwaite."

Chapter Sixteen

S ERENA, WHO WAS happy to face up to any number of spies, bullies, blackmailers, and murderers, was not yet ready to meet her mother. Or even Gervaise. Caught on the wrong foot, in direct contravention of their instructions when they sent her out of London, she was all but hosting a moonlight party beneath their home and waltzing in the arms of an eccentric artist who was probably also a rake. Moreover, her sisters were present.

And there was no chance of keeping the last fact quiet, for they ran at their brother with great enthusiasm. "Gervaise! Mama! We didn't know you were coming!"

That must have been only too glaringly obvious.

"Chin up," Tamar breathed. "Allow me to escort you to them."

Well, perhaps Tamar would be one too many blows and reduce them to silence. She clutched his arm gratefully.

As they hurried through the dancers, Serena saw Mrs. Winslow approach her mother and brother, much as she had every other guest coming from the cliff path. Her greeting must have included an explanation of some kind, absolving Serena of actually hosting the event, for a faintly mollified look entered Braithwaite's face at least.

"Our letters can only just have reached London," Tamar said quietly. "This isn't in response. They must have crossed with them on the road."

"Then they don't know," Serena said, in craven relief that she could at least leave that until tomorrow.

"No," Tamar agreed, with a quick glance over his shoulder at the man who'd accosted him just as she'd glimpsed her mother. He was following them.

Please, God, don't let him be some kind of constable or Bow Street Runner...

"Mama, what a wonderful surprise," she said, embracing her mother's rigid person before turning to her brother. "Gervaise. Allow me to present you to Lord Tamar. My lord, may I present my mother, the Dowager Countess of Braithwaite, and my brother the earl. Mama, this is Lord Tamar, who—"

She got no further.

"You *are* Lord Tamar," pronounced the strange man who'd accosted him a few moments ago. Insinuating himself in front of Tamar, he produced from his shoulder bag a large bundle tied in a piece of cloth. "From Captain Alban. Payment in full, he says." He dumped the bundle in Tamar's bewildered arms, ripping off the string that tied it to reveal a heap of coins, jewels, watches, enamel boxes, and silver picture frames.

The man grinned, tugged his forelock, and effaced himself.

Tamar began to laugh, a soft, helpless sound that in any other circumstances would have had her joining in. As it was, she couldn't help demanding, "Why is Captain Alban sending you...treasure?"

"Because I called him a damned pirate—I beg your pardon, a *dashed* pirate. Trust me, it's a good joke, although I'll allow his timing could be better." It certainly couldn't have been worse. He was meeting her mother and brother for the first time, in possession of what looked alarmingly like stolen goods.

"You'd best bring it up to the castle," Serena said, aware of many curious eyes on the treasure *and* on the somewhat strained family reunion.

"It is somewhat late for visitors, Serena," her mother said forbiddingly, and turned on her heels.

"Nevertheless," Tamar said, "I hope you'll forgive my taking one minute of your time before I leave."

The countess didn't turn back, and Miss Grey led her charges silently after her. All three girls glanced at Tamar and Serena as they passed. Helen even mouthed a silent, *Good luck.*

"Why?" Braithwaite asked, meeting Tamar's gaze.

Serena held her breath.

"Because I wish to marry Lady Serena," Tamar said boldly.

Frowning, as if trying to dredge up from his memory exactly who Lord Tamar was, Braithwaite waved him and Serena ahead of himself.

WITHOUT A WORD to Serena, Braithwaite threw open a door off the main hall. "If you please, sir," he invited Tamar.

Serena cast him an anxious glance. About to bear, no doubt, all the fury of her mother's verbal assault, she cared more, clearly, for the result of his interview with Braithwaite. And Tamar could see no way that was going to go well. His best hope, for now, was to avoid outright refusal and prevent Braithwaite hating him.

With a murmur of thanks, he walked past the earl, who couldn't have been more than four of five years older than Tamar, and into a study.

Braithwaite did not invite him to sit. "Forgive me, I couldn't quite place the name when my sister introduced you. Now that I have, I am even more surprised to receive your offer. I do you the honor of assuming it to be a serious offer."

"For Lady Serena? I have never been more serious in my life."

"Again, forgive me, this question is inspired largely by hearsay, but do you have the means to support my sister? Do you even have a home?"

"I have a large home with a few rooms that are still livable. I earn a little money from painting and have reason to believe that could increase consid—"

"Painting?" Braithwaite interrupted with utmost scorn. His gaze all but lashed the bundle hanging at Tamar's side.

"Painting," Tamar repeated. "This is payment for such, albeit jocular—"

"From Captain Alban. So I heard. A man whose wealth is hardly above reproach. And I believe you have dependents?"

He was hammering it home, damn him. The outright refusal would not be long in coming. Perhaps he should have left Serena to speak to him first, but that wouldn't have sat well with Tamar.

"One of my sisters is married. I have another and two brothers. I would also point out that my name and my title are among the oldest and highest in the country."

Braithwaite scowled. "If it weren't for your rank, sir, I would not even have done you the courtesy of this interview. In effect, you offer my sister nothing, and I would be failing in my duties as her guardian if I listened further. I must decline your offer and insist you break off all contact with my sister. I bid you good night."

A surge of temper fought with the knowledge that Braithwaite was right in all his assessments. He had nothing, except Serena's love, and if her own brother could not see the importance of that... But there was nothing else for it tonight, but to leave.

So, keeping the rage and humiliation from his face, he merely bowed and walked out of the room. Paton, with the faintest look of sympathy, was waiting to see him out.

He thought, briefly, of returning to the party on the beach and getting blind drunk. But in truth, this would hardly help his cause, and whatever Braithwaite thought at this moment, Tamar had no intention of giving up. Since he suspected Braithwaite was watching him from the study window, he walked toward the main drive with as much dignity as he could muster.

SERENA FOLLOWED HER mother upstairs with reluctance. What she really wished to do was listen at the study door. Or at least follow her younger sisters and Miss Grey to their rooms.

"Serena, I have no words," the countess said with blatant untruth as she closed the door of the small drawing room and turned to face her. "I am appalled! My last instructions to you were to live in quiet isolation, without visiting or receiving. And the first things I see when I come home—and ironically, I came especially to relax those conditions—is a party on the castle doorstep with you at the center, capering around the beach with some ill-dressed stranger! Worse, you dragged your young sisters into the vulgar escapade."

"Vulgar? Oh, Mama, no, it was truly quite unexceptionable! You must have seen that. Mrs. Winslow and Mrs. Grant arranged everything, and all the most respectable people were there, even the vicar. In truth, it was arranged to cheer poor Catherine who has had an unpleasant disappointment—"

"That may be." The countess sank heavily into her favorite armchair. "But I had thought better of Kate Grant than to encourage your attendance before she had even received my permission!"

"To be sure, she did not encourage me," Serena said at once. "She has merely looked after me."

"Looked after you? With some down-at-heel nobody having the insolence to ask for your hand before he has even stepped over the door? And I have to say, I'm shocked to see your sisters on terms of intimacy with him—"

"Mama, he is not nobody." Impetuously, Serena came to stand before her mother. "He is the Marquis of Tamar and so ranks above us if you care for such things!"

"I don't," the countess retorted. "Not with that name and that history. You can be sure Braithwaite will send him about his business. More importantly, since I doubt this offer sprang out of nowhere, I must suppose this is not the first party you have attended since your return."

"Well, no," Serena admitted. "You know about the Assembly Room ball."

"And when I question the servants—as you may be sure I shall—will I discover that this man has called on you here?"

Serena met her gaze with difficulty. "He has been here," she said cautiously. "To paint the girls—fully chaperoned by Miss Grey and Mrs. Grant."

Her mother's eyes showed an alarming tendency to pop. Her fist clenched on the arm of her chair. "I had thought better of Kate Crowmore. She was always wild, but I imagined there was a saving sweetness in her. I never cut her. I always defended her. Why she should now repay me by ruining my family—"

"Mama, you're being ridiculous!" Serena interrupted, swirling away to throw herself into the chair opposite. "There is more, here, as I wrote to you—or perhaps it was to Gervaise. At any rate, you must both have left London before the letter reached you. We were obliged to look after Lord Tamar when he was shot defending us from French spies!"

The door opened in time for her brother to hear this announcement as he strode in and shoved the door closed again behind him. "For God's sake, Serena, no more stories! You know you were in the wrong—"

"To care for a man who was shot in front of home? Defending it, defending my sisters and me, from the enemy? Even you, even Mama, would have given him a bed and sent for the doctor! Which is exactly what I did! And the very next day, when I was abducted by Valère—who pretended to be an emigre nobleman but was in fact a Bonapartist spy and the man who disappointed Catherine besides—when I was taken by him to let him blow up the Black Fort and free the prisoners-of-war, it was Tamar who saved me! The debt of gratitude we all bear him is boundless!"

"You're talking nonsense, Serena," her mother said coldly.

"I understand you wish to excuse yourself from ill behavior—" Braithwaite began.

"Ask Mr. Winslow," Serena interrupted. "Ask Major Doverton. Ask the servants, Miss Grey, my sisters, since everyone else's word clearly counts above mine."

At least their sudden pause gave her a certain furious satisfaction.

"You know such things exist here," she said contemptuously.

"Spies tried to take Gillie during our spring ball if you recall, and if Wickenden hadn't been there, who knows what might have happened to her? *My* safety, on the other hand, is obviously of less importance than the fact that my savior is poor!"

They both stared at her.

"You mean this is *true?*" the countess blurted.

"Were you hurt?" Braithwaite demanded.

"Not to speak of, though my courage did quail until I saw Tamar had brought Jem and the others—"

Braithwaite dragged his hand through his hair, frowning direly. He sank onto the sofa. "This is...outrageous. Be sure I will extend all gratitude and..." He trailed off, then lifted his frowning gaze to Serena's. "But still, you must admit that you do not know who he is! The chances of him actually *being* the marquis are remote. No one has seen any of the family in decades, not since the old marquis died. He could be any flim flam man—"

"He is Tamar," Serena interrupted unwarily. "Lord Daxton knows him. They were at school together."

In retrospect, Daxton's was the wrong name to mention.

"Daxton," the countess repeated with loathing.

"I wondered when his name would come up," Brathwaite said bitterly. "Last month you were in love with him and this month you expect us to believe—"

Serena wanted to scream. "I was never remotely in love with Lord Daxton! Which is fortunate, because he is certainly not in love with me! I *danced* with him. Tamar is...different."

Braithwaite looked maddeningly superior. "And you seriously believe you love him? After an acquaintance of what, two weeks? Three?"

"It makes no difference," she said simply. "If you don't like him, I'm sorry for it. But I can't live without him and I won't."

"Go to your room, Serena," the countess said, clearly revolted.

IT WAS ONLY just light and there was a faint frost on the ground as Serena crept out of the side-door and hurried across to the orchard. She hadn't slept much during the night, anger and outrage on Tamar's behalf, alternating with sadness and frustration and sheer longing.

New fallen leaves crunched under her feet, making it difficult to walk silently. There was a crackle to her right, she turned and walked straight into Tamar's arms. Her hood fell back and she met his kiss.

She clung to him. "This is where I belong," she whispered against his lips.

"Was it awful?" he asked.

"Nothing I didn't expect. I just didn't imagine I would feel so...*angry*. What of you? Was Brathwaite mean?"

"No meaner than I would have been in his shoes. Cold would describe him better."

"He isn't really like that," Serena said apologetically. "I think he just feels compelled to protect me and does it the wrong way. Besides, knowing Gervaise, he is already feeling guilty over Maynard. We were never a good match, and he did promote it, though I had the last word. Guilt was at the root of his sending me home from London, too, even if he doesn't know it."

"At least you weren't locked in your chamber."

"Yet," she said wryly.

He touched her cheek. "Thank you for giving me this morning."

She smiled. "Did you think I wouldn't?" Even as the words left her lips, she saw that was exactly what he'd thought. Or at least feared. She drove her fingers through his hair. "How could you?"

"They are your family and I know you love them."

"I love you, too. That doesn't mean I shall always give in to you when we're married. Especially not when you're wrong."

He let out a breath of laughter and kissed her again.

She pressed her cheek to his, loving its rough warmth. "I haven't given up," she assured him. "I'm still working on them. Already Gervaise is impressed by your feats against the spies. I believe he will write to you expressing his gratitude and appreciation. And then, you know, once they speak to Blackhaven people and see how you are liked and accepted everywhere, they will soften further."

"I could wish Alban hadn't set his man on me with his damned treasure," Tamar said. "Especially not at that precise moment. Your brother thinks me a thief and a pirate."

"I know." Laughter caught in her throat. "Though it *was* funny."

He grinned. "And not very useful. I'll be afraid to sell the stuff, in case people think it's stolen. Still, I did find this." He fished something from his pocket and opened his fingers to reveal a pretty sapphire and diamond ring. "I thought it was the color of your eyes,"

Swallowing a lump in her throat, she held out her hand and watched him slide the ring over her finger. "Thank you," she whispered. She didn't need such trinkets, but she understood how much it meant to him that he could make her such a gift, even from Alban's joke.

They talked a little longer, and he told her about an idea he had to take his seat in the House and become active in the political scene. "Perhaps not this year or next, but soon, depending on how things turn out."

"Instead of painting?" She would be sorry for that.

"Oh no," he said. "As well as that. I spend a lot of time painting dross, you know. If I only painted what truly inspired me—or what made me money—I would have plenty of time left over for other purposes."

"Hmm. I think your idea of dross and mine might be different. But it is an excellent notion and one that might impress Gervaise, who has also begun a political career." She glanced up at the sky. "I had better go in," she said reluctantly. "Or my mother will send someone to look for me."

He kissed her one last time and let her go. There was pain in leaving him, for she didn't know how long she would get away with these assignations.

Hurrying indoors, she left her cloak in her chamber and went down to breakfast where she discovered her mother had just joined the girls and Miss Grey. It was a custom Serena had begun, for she saw no reason why her sisters should be banished to the schoolroom for family meals. She herself had hated such banishment. And so far, at least, the countess had not objected.

"Good morning," Serena said brightly, kissing her mother's cheek before going to fill her plate from the sideboard. "I thought you might sleep longer after your journey."

"I barely slept at all," her mother returned. "Not with all this nonsense about spies and moonlit revels, and painting marquises!"

"Lord Tamar?" Helen said at once. "He's very good. You should ask him to show you our picture."

"Which I suppose I'm paying for," Gervaise said sardonically, coming into the room in time to hear.

"Not if you don't want to," Serena retorted. "I will buy it with my pin money."

Sleep had clearly not improved her brother's sympathies or his temper. "Oh, for the love of God, Serena, can't you see that whatever he might have done for you on the spur of the moment, he is a charlatan?"

"Because his clothes are a little threadbare?" she shot back, throwing herself into the chair beside Maria. "Because what little money he gets from his remaining estate goes back into it, or simply feeds his family?"

Braithwaite snatched up a plate and glowered at her. "No. Because there is no proof he even is Tamar. Because he receives plunder from notorious pirates like Alban—"

"Captain Alban is in fact a hero who's given the French many a bloody nose," Serena retorted. "Besides which, Alban is his Christian name, and he is in fact a Lamont of Roseley, a neighbor of ours, and is married, moreover to Lady Arabella Niven!"

The countess sniffed. "If you ask me, it's suspicious he changed his name. The Lamont boy was always trouble, but he is not our concern here."

"Well, I shall not listen to your traducing Lord Tamar either. I love him."

Her voice caught on the last words, and Braithwaite's face softened as he sat opposite her and set down his loaded plate. "Serena, have you really considered this? Even if he is who says he is, and no matter how charming you find him—I will allow him to be personable in his own way—there is bad blood in the Tamars. How would he support you? Where would you live? He has nothing."

"I have money."

"The world knows that, Serena," her mother said tartly. "You may be assured he does, too."

"Oh, we're beyond all that," Serena exclaimed. "Just spend some time with him and you will see—"

The countess sniffed again. "I hardly think that will be necessary."

Maria pressed her foot over Serena's, warning her to be silent, not to provoke them further. So, she took a deep breath and ate her breakfast.

"I thought I would call on Mr. Winslow this morning," Braithwaite said at last. "Perhaps, Mama, you and Serena would care to accompany me?"

"I think my first business is with Kate Grant," the countess said ominously. "Serena may come with *me*. In fact, she had better, so I may keep my eye on her!"

Chapter Seventeen

LORD BRAITHWAITE RODE away from the Winslows feeling appalled by the danger Serena had faced with the French spies, and inevitably proud of her spirited reaction, however much greater a risk she'd taken. And although he was more grateful than ever for what Tamar had contributed to her rescue, he couldn't help being further appalled by Winslow's opinion of him.

"Oh, there's no doubt he's the marquis," the squire had told him. "Sir Henry Horsham knew old Tamar well, and even recognized the son. And Lord Daxton, among others, knew him as a child. Likeable chap. Accepted everywhere, and a damned fine painter, to boot. Sadly, he doesn't have two pennies to rub together, but that must be laid at his father's door."

"Then Mrs. Winslow receives him?"

"Oh yes." He glanced shrewdly at Braithwaite. "Though I wouldn't want him for Catherine."

In many ways, it would have been so much easier if the man had simply been an imposter, a flim-flam man after Serena's fortune. Of course, the real Tamar was after her fortune, too, but it wasn't so easy to dismiss a marquis as a cheat and a liar. Especially not after he'd saved her life.

In some dismay, he rode into Blackhaven to call on Major Doverton and get the military perspective on what had occurred. That didn't help either, for Doverton had nothing but praise for Tamar's courage.

"Clever chap, too," he added. "He'd have made a fine officer—

sound tactician *and* strategist."

"I wonder why he didn't join up," Brathwaite said. It would surely have been a reliable source of income if nothing else.

"I asked him that. He told me he couldn't afford the commission, and besides, didn't have the discipline."

"Well," Braithwaite said, offering his hand. "I know he couldn't have rescued my sister without you. You have my eternal gratitude, and my mother's. And if there's ever any way in which I can be of service to you, you need only ask."

Churning him up as he left Doverton, was the growing knowledge that he was going to have to call on Tamar, too, and offer proper thanks. He thought it might choke him. But the man had almost died to save Doverton, and had risked himself again while still wounded to save Serena.

Fortunately, he had no idea where Tamar was staying. Until he ran into the vicar, who had stopped to chat to Bernard Muir and his stepmother outside the coffee house. They all greeted him in friendly spirit, and he bowed to Mrs. Muir, asking civilly after her health and her infant son.

As the conversation moved swiftly on, Braithwaite dropped in the fact that his sisters wished him to buy a painting from Lord Tamar. He thought it quite a subtle way to discover the marquis's dirty linen, for Bernard and the vicar would know everyone, and Mrs. Muir was even stricter about the proprieties than his mother.

"You could do worse," Bernard assured him cheerfully. "Everyone wants one of Tamar's daubs on their wall."

"I'm not sure I want a *daub* of my sisters," Braithwaite objected.

"The gallery has some of his work," the vicar observed. "Or you could step round to his studio—one of the fishermen's cottages along from the harbor."

Damnation. Now he had no excuse. Grant caught his eye and gave a quick, sympathetic smile, almost as if he knew what was in Braithwaite's head. The living of Blackhaven was within Braithwaite's gift, and he'd been happy to approve Grant for the position. He was gentlemanly, clever, and compassionate, and everyone seemed to like him. Including wicked Kate Crowmore who'd married him. Braithwaite began to wonder if he'd made a mistake.

"I must go," the vicar said now. "But I shall be free for luncheon if you'd care to call at the vicarage."

"I believe my mother and sister are already descending upon your wife," Braithwaite said.

"Excellent. I'll hope to see your lordship, too. Good morning."

Left with no excuse, Braithwaite dragged his feet to the end of High Street and walked through the market to the harbor. Surely, he had grace enough to thank a stranger—a fellow nobleman who had not been born with quite so much luck as himself—for saving the life of his sister? He could even explain further why the match was impossible. Without being quite so insulting to his rank as he had been last night when he hadn't believed the man was really the Marquis of Tamar.

Braithwaite turned along the row of fishermen's cottages, wondering which Tamar used. In fact, he hoped Tamar wasn't there, when without warning, the door he was passing flew open and two vaguely familiar gentlemen were all but pushed out.

"Shove off, there's good fellows," came Tamar's voice. "I'm working."

"Dash it, Tamar!" said one of them indignantly, waving a brandy flask before his friend dragged him off and Braithwaite had a clear view of the marquis, tousled and disreputable in his shirt sleeves, spattered with paint of various hues.

He was in the midst of calling some amusing insult after his friends when his gaze caught Braithwaite and the words died on his lips.

"My lord," Braithwaite said, bowing stiffly.

"My lord," Tamar returned, just a shade sardonically. He stepped back from the door. "Please step inside if you don't mind the mess. I'm afraid tidiness is not one of my virtues."

That was an understatement. The tiny one-roomed cottage was stuffed full of boxes and easels and abandoned clothing, the walls lined with hung paintings while more were piled against them on the floor. Only the window appeared to be clear and clean, and Braithwaite could see why. The view over the sea was spectacular.

Braithwaite stepped over a box of paints, and Tamar brushed past him to shove a blanket and coat off the couch onto the floor.

"Sit, if you wish," he offered casually. "Glass of ale? I've had to fob those fellows off with the last of the brandy."

"No, I thank you," Braithwaite said. He found a small space beside two covered easels opposite the couch. "I shan't keep you. I only wished to convey to you my thanks. I have heard the part you played in thwarting the French attack on the fort, and more particularly, in rescuing my sister."

"No thanks are necessary. My reasons were largely selfish, with care for my country a rather poor second."

"Whatever your reasons," Braithwaite said with difficulty, "I am in your debt. And you should know I value what you did."

Tamar smiled, throwing himself on to the couch. "But only up to a point. Not enough to permit me to address your sister."

"You're not a stupid man, by all accounts," Braithwaite said. "You must know my reasons. Nor can they come as any surprise to you."

"No," Tamar admitted. His lips twisted. "Believe it or not, I once had the same scruples, until I saw how unhappy Serena was when I acted upon them. I want her to be happy, and for some reason that is beyond both of us, that has to include me."

"I have no doubt of her genuine attachment," Braithwaite said stiffly. "But it is not lasting. Your acquaintance is too short."

"I understand you, but you're wrong," Tamar said in tones of certainty.

"For God's sake man, this is not just your studio, you *sleep* here!" Braithwaite burst out. "Do you truly expect my sister to live in such squalor?"

"No, though she's welcome to if she wishes. My hope is that within a month or two I shall be able to afford a decent set of rooms, or perhaps a cottage outside Blackhaven."

"How?" Braithwaite demanded rudely, his eyes straying to the paintings on the wall beside him. Eye-catching seascapes, full of motion and atmosphere, not vulgar but not, to his eyes, outstanding either.

Tamar shrugged. "I can sell a few more paintings at a higher price."

"And add that to your treasure from Alban?"

Tamar laughed. "Captain Alban is a gentleman and a wealthy shipowner. If there were truly acts of piracy in his past—and I know nothing about that—he has no need to resort to such now. I'll wager you this roof over my head that none of these items were stolen."

Braithwaite turned aside impatiently, and his coat brushed against the easel beside him, catching the cloth which covered it.

To his surprise, Tamar made an instinctive dive off the couch to catch the falling cloth. Instead, he upset the balance of both easels and both cloths slipped to the floor. Tamar only just managed to steady one easel while Braithwaite seized the other...and found himself gazing into Serena's eyes.

At first glance, the painting was a stunningly perfect likeness, so much so that he immediately looked at the other to see if it was even half so good.

It was the back of Serena's head, apparently the reverse of the first picture. Sunlight seemed to glow from every individual strand of her hair and the simple knot in which it was tied, revealing the delicate curve of her neck and shoulders beneath. Although there was nothing as obvious or as blasphemous as a halo, that was one of Braithwaite's overall impressions, swiftly followed by an appealing mixture of innocence and sensuality. And mystery, because even the sun seemed to love her. And yet, although you were desperate to, you could not see her face.

Until you looked at the other painting. In the same autumnal, leafy setting—which seemed vaguely familiar to Braithwaite, although he didn't even try to place it at that moment—Serena's full beauty dazzled him. It wasn't just that the artist had caught her humor, cleverness, and sweetness in one characteristic expression, it was that every delicate line of her face and gown and posture shouted her sheer vitality, her love of life and the world. The painter had known Serena well, and more than that...

"I don't know if they're finished," Tamar said with unexpected nervousness. "I always cover them up for at least a day, so I can see afresh if something needs to change."

More than that...

"Don't," Braithwaite blurted. "Don't change anything." Slowly, he raised his gaze from the painting to the painter. *More than that...* "You love her."

"Yes."

Braithwaite drew in his breath, trying to deal with what this meant, with turning everything on its head and looking at it afresh. "Perhaps I will have that ale."

Tamar went and poured it and placed it in his hands. He drank it down, then set the cup back on the cluttered table and picked up his hat. "Come with me," he instructed, then paused. "If you please."

"I please," Tamar replied, apparently amused. He shook out the coat he'd abandoned on the floor and shrugged himself into it before grabbing a necktie that dangled from one of the pictures on the wall. He wound it carelessly around his throat while heading for the door.

"That's my orchard," Braithwaite said suddenly. "In your pictures."

"Yes, it is," Tamar agreed, locking the door behind them. "I'm afraid I've been in the habit of trespassing in your grounds to paint. Serena caught me there. That was how I first met her."

HER MOTHER TOOK so long to prepare for the expedition to Blackhaven that Serena almost gave up on it. In the end, she only persevered because she felt obliged to give Kate what protection she could.

And then, when they finally arrived before the vicarage and dismounted from the carriage, the maid told them her mistress was not at home.

The countess stared. "I am not accustomed to being kept waiting."

Clearly, she suspected Kate of deliberately denying herself. The maid looked distinctly flustered, her gaze flying to Serena for help.

"Of course," Serena said, remembering. "This is one of Mrs. Grant's soup-kitchen days. I believe I promised to help her, too, so I hope she'll forgive me! Might we wait for her to come home?"

"Of course, m'lady," the maid said in some relief. "Go into the parlor and I'll bring tea."

Mollified, the countess condescended to enter the house and wait. Which would at least give poor Kate warning of who had descended upon her. In fact, they didn't have long to wait before Kate and Mr. Grant both came into the house, laughing together at something.

Serena's mother sniffed with disapproval. Voices could be heard in the hall as the maid, no doubt, explained the presence of guests. Without delay, Kate entered the parlor, and came straight to the countess with her hand held out.

"Lady Braithwaite, how wonderful! I glimpsed you last night, so I knew you were back. May I present my husband, Tristram Grant."

Kate's natural manner probably did more than anything else to convince the countess that no crime had been committed. However, she wouldn't have been Serena's mother if she hadn't launched into a criticism of Kate taking upon herself the role of chaperone to Serena before she had been given permission.

"Be fair, Mama," Serena argued. "You know I would have been driven mad, or got into quite horrendous trouble through boredom if I hadn't been allowed to go anywhere!"

"It seems to me you still did!" her mother snapped.

"On the contrary," Mr. Grant said gently. "I believe Lady Serena behaves at all times like the lady you wish her to be. My wife merely lent her company for the benefit of a critical world—even when that meant travelling up to the fort in the pouring rain to face armed enemy spies."

It was quite masterly, Serena allowed, absolving both herself and Kate from any blame whatsoever, and reminding Lady Braithwaite that she owed Kate not criticism but gratitude.

Serena's mother stared at him.

"Ah, look," Kate said brightly. "Here is Lord Braithwaite arriving, too…with Lord Tamar."

The blood drained from Serena's face so fast she was glad to be sitting down. "Together?" she asked anxiously.

"Apparently so." Kate met her gaze with a resigned quirk of the eyebrows.

"You will not go near him," Serena's mother hissed in her ear. "You will stay by my side at all times."

Serena didn't answer. She was too alarmed by what the two men might have said to each other that they were coming to the Grants at the same time. Were they coming to ask Mr. Grant to mediate? Or, more likely, to try and force Tamar to renounce her face to face. He wouldn't, of course, but his refusal would lead to such unpleasantness.

Well, they could still escape to Scotland.

She was afraid to breathe.

The parlor door opened in unusual silence, and both gentleman, the one so exquisitely dressed and the other so shabby, bowed to the room in general. Tamar sought her eyes. He didn't seem terribly worried, but then he rarely did. It all went on beneath the surface with him.

Both Kate and her husband shook hands with both lords.

"Very glad to see you both," Mr. Grant pronounced. "Have you come for luncheon, or did you want to speak to me about something else?"

"I want you to call the banns," Braithwaite said, stunning the room. "For Serena and Tamar here."

Serena's mouth fell open.

"*What?*" her mother exclaimed. "Braithwaite, have you taken leave of your senses?"

Tamar was staring at him, pulling his ear as if he was afraid he'd heard wrongly.

"Of course not," Braithwaite said. "Quite the opposite in fact."

"Hold on," Tamar said. "Are you actually giving us permission to marry?"

Braithwaite's eyebrows shot up in surprise. "Yes. Didn't I say?"

Serena's paralysis broke. An instant before her reacted, she flew out of her chair and into Tamar's waiting arms. Before them all, his mouth crushed hers in an exuberant, enthusiastic kiss that had her mother moaning for her smelling salts.

Emerging breathless and slightly tousled, she caught her brother's arm, smiling. "Thank you, Gervaise."

He inclined his head ironically.

"What changed your mind?" she asked curiously.

"He loves you." Braithwaite flushed slightly as everyone stared at him. "More than that, he *knows* you and *still* loves you."

Serena punched his arm without anger. "Yes, but how do *you* know?"

"I saw his painting," Braithwaite said. "Both his paintings of you."

Tamar loosened his grip on Serena though he still held her with one arm around her waist. "You got all of that from the paintings?"

Braithwaite nodded curtly.

Tamar let out a breath of laughter. "By God, I *am* good!"

Chapter Eighteen

THREE WEEKS LATER, Lady Serena Conway married Rupert Alan Gaunt, eighth Marquis of Tamar, in St. Andrew's Church at Blackhaven.

Serena, who'd never in her wildest dreams imagined that the wedding would happen so quickly unless they eloped to Scotland, went through the ceremony in something of a daze. It was intended as a private wedding, with only her family present. Tamar hadn't troubled to invite his own siblings since "we'd only have the whole pack of them up here sponging." She suspected his real reason had more to do with the expense of traveling. And Julian, of course, had only just been sent home.

In fact, there were less family members than Serena had hoped, since Frances had just given birth to a son and wasn't fit to travel. On the other hand, Lord Daxton and his new wife—who seemed to be known universally as Lady Dax—had appeared to support the groom, as had the famous Captain Alban and his aristocratic wife. Kate Grant and the Winslows also turned out to witness the event. The rest of the church was packed with Braithwaite people and as many Blackhaven townspeople as could fit through the open doors.

Deliriously happy, Serena smiled at everyone, especially her grinning and slightly smug little sisters, and clung to her new husband's arm as they walked out of the church as man and wife. Tamar looked wildly handsome in a smart new suit of clothes bought for the occasion, while Serena wore her favorite white trimmed gown with dark red.

An impromptu wedding feast had been set up under canopies, for the tenants and estate workers, while the "quality" breakfasted in the castle dining room.

Serena knew she chattered and laughed her way through the meal, though she had no recollection of what she said or what amused her. She seemed to be only aware of Tamar by her side.

Then, quite suddenly, it came to her. Laughter gurgled into her throat. She lowered her voice. "I've just realized I'm the Marchioness of Tamar. I have precedence over my mother!"

"I knew there was a reason you married me."

"That must be it," she agreed happily.

He smiled while his eyes darkened thrillingly. "I can't wait to show you a few other reasons."

Although she flushed, she lifted her chin in challenge. "On the cellar floor?"

"Or under the apple tree."

"Or in our rooms, hurriedly refurbished by my favorite brother for our use."

"Or there. The location is really immaterial."

And suddenly, she wanted everyone gone, leaving the two of them alone together. Braithwaite was returning to London tomorrow and taking their mother with him. They would truly have the place to themselves...if one didn't count the children. And Miss Grey. And the servants.

But soon enough, Tamar suggested they could leave. There was no wedding trip to be waved off on, so they were merely applauded through the Long Gallery, after which Serena led him along the passages into the older part of the castle where her bedchamber had been for years, and where other rooms had been made available for them to live in relative privacy.

"Until Tamar Abbey is ready for you," Braithwaite had said.

It was a huge job. As a wedding gift, Braithwaite had made available his own surveyors and engineers and provided funds to begin the repairs, to make at least part of the Abbey habitable. This left Serena's money to live on for the time being and to plough into the estate along with whatever Tamar could make. He was optimistic this would all lead to a greater yield from the estate in the long term and neither Braithwaite nor Braithwaite's steward disagreed with him. Even Dax, who, seemed to know a bizarre amount about farming, had offered encouragement and advice.

Tamar took her hand, and together, they walked into their sitting room. The connecting door to her bedchamber had once been kept locked, as had the door to the room on the other side, which was now made into a dressing room for Tamar.

"What do you think?" she asked anxiously as she showed him through the rooms. "Do you like them? Will they do for now?"

"They'll more than do, Serena. Come here."

Suddenly shy, she found herself blushing as she walked across the bedchamber and into his arms. His kiss was tender and thorough, and the hovering butterflies in her stomach seemed to take flight.

He lifted his head, gazing at the wall beside the window. "You hung my picture by your bed."

"I was being selfish. I know more people should see it, but I wanted to go to sleep and wake up with it every morning. It seemed the next best thing to having you here."

He took her face between his hands. "What did I ever do to deserve you in my life?" he said softly, and kissed her again as she slipped her arms around his waist.

She imagined his hands shook slightly as he pulled the pins from her hair and unfastened her gown with rather more efficiency than was quite seemly in a man.

Besides, it was still light outside.

She dragged her mouth free with a gasp. "Why don't you go to the other room and—"

"No," he said uncompromisingly, and took back her mouth.

Desire flamed through her. She pressed closer to him, emitting a tiny moan of hunger when she felt the hardness of his erection. His knee pushed between her legs and his thigh stroked the hot, heavy place she most needed his touch. Her mouth opened wider, and he plundered it with ruthless sensuality.

Somehow her gown, petticoat, and stays slipped to the floor around her feet. One of his hands swept down her back to her bottom, holding her closer into him while his other hand found her breast and caressed.

Her whole body trembled. And then her shift followed the rest of her clothes and she stood fully naked in his arms.

His breathing was more labored than hers. "Oh, Christ," he muttered. "You are beautiful."

He snatched her up in his arms and strode with her to the bed. As she landed on her back, he tore off his coat and necktie, then kicked off his shoes and swung himself over her. Holding most of his weight on his elbows, he pinned her lower body with his hips while he kissed her mouth and throat and breasts.

Totally awash with sensation, she found herself scrabbling beneath his shirt to feel the hot velvet of his skin. Impatiently, he pulled the shirt up over his head and threw it aside. She rose up with him, flattening her palms over his chest in wonder, caressing.

Slowly, gently, he pushed her back, and she saw that his lower clothes had gone, too. She had a glimpse of his manhood, huge and strangely thrilling, and then he lay on her once more, his mouth seducing all over again as his hands played over her body and found the heat between her thighs.

She cried out when he entered her body, but only with surprise. The minor discomfort was nothing like the pain her mother had warned her about, and even that began to vanish as he moved in her. She clung to him, following in blind, desperate hunger. His voice shook as he told her over and over of her beauty and how much he loved and desired her. And then his whole body trembled, and so did hers as the building pleasure galloped out of control and swept her away in a tide so intense she thought she would never recover.

His blissful groans filled her ears as he collapsed upon her. She held him to her, seeking his mouth, and he gave it in a wild, gasping kiss.

Rocked to her core, Serena listened to their heartbeats gradually slow.

"That," she whispered, "must have been what I wanted all along."

"It's certainly what I've wanted."

"And now that you've had it, are you satisfied?"

He smiled. "Only for the next three minutes."

She couldn't help the shocked widening of her eyes. "You mean we may do it again?"

"Oh yes," he said fervently. He stroked her hair and smiled down at her. She could not doubt the pleasure he'd taken in her. It made her proud, almost triumphant. "But since I'm looking after you, not until morning."

WHEN TAMAR WOKE in the morning, she wasn't in the bed. He'd wakened several times during the night, his limbs wrapped around her soft, delicious body and only by superhuman effort had he prevented himself from taking her again. Especially when she'd pushed back into him, encouraging him. To save her, he'd made love to her with his mouth, and his own painful frustration had drowned in delight at her pleasure.

But in daylight, he missed her. He sat up. Through the open bed curtains, he saw her standing at the window in her night rail, waving. The rumble of carriage wheels and the clop of horses' hooves on stone drifted up to him. Throwing off the covers, he rose and walked to the window, drawing her back against his naked body. She smiled, nestling into him.

"Is someone coming or going?" he asked.

"Gervaise and Mama, returning to London."

"You mean we have the whole castle to ourselves?"

"Apart from the children, Miss Grey, and the servants."

"Who will all be busy."

"Edwards brought us coffee," Serena offered. "Would you like some?"

"I'd love some." He was busy searching his way beneath her nightgown as he drew her away from the window. She twisted her head around and kissed him so sweetly that he forgot about the coffee in his urgency.

"And then," she said breathlessly, wickedly. "And then, at some point during the day, would you like to finally make good your threat and take me on the cellar floor?"

He gave a shout of laughter. "Yes, damn it, I would."

And he did.

Mary Lancaster's Newsletter

If you enjoyed *The Wicked Marquis*, and would like to keep up with Mary's new releases and other book news, please sign up to Mary's mailing list to receive her occasional Newsletter.

http://eepurl.com/b4Xoif

Other Books by Mary Lancaster

VIENNA WALTZ (The Imperial Season, Book 1)
VIENNA WOODS (The Imperial Season, Book 2)
VIENNA DAWN (The Imperial Season, Book 3)
THE WICKED BARON (Blackhaven Brides, Book 1)
THE WICKED LADY (Blackhaven Brides, Book 2)
THE WICKED REBEL (Blackhaven Brides, Book 3)
THE WICKED HUSBAND (Blackhaven Brides, Book 4)
REBEL OF ROSS
A PRINCE TO BE FEARED: the love story of Vlad Dracula
AN ENDLESS EXILE
A WORLD TO WIN

About Mary Lancaster

Mary Lancaster's first love was historical fiction. Her other passions include coffee, chocolate, red wine and black and white films – simultaneously where possible. She hates housework.

As a direct consequence of the first love, she studied history at St. Andrews University. She now writes full time at her seaside home in Scotland, which she shares with her husband, three children and a small, crazy dog.

Connect with Mary on-line:

Email Mary:
Mary@MaryLancaster.com

Website:
www.MaryLancaster.com

Newsletter sign-up:
http://eepurl.com/b4Xoif

Facebook Author Page:
facebook.com/MaryLancasterNovelist

Facebook Timeline:
facebook.com/mary.lancaster.1656

Printed in Great Britain
by Amazon

38770075R00119